The Golden Bed of th[...]

By Mark Acraman

I dedicate this book to the next Einstein, that undoubtably spent his or her entire life stacking shelves. To the next Mozart, that never learnt to play music as they were too tired from working back-to-back shifts for minimum wage. I dedicate this book to the oppressive system that protects the status quo for the few while exploiting the masses.

What a species we could be...

Remember How the Flowers Looked When You Were Young

I raised my delicate chin and glanced my virgin eyes to the night sky. A wrought chasm; vast ocean, model of treasures, perpetual beauty. Never still, never moving. Never black, never white. The air tasted so thin and so brittle. I took a deep breath and was transported far away, to some place where the air is warm all the time and the stress and malevolence of the world doesn't seem to apply to those playing their small part in a small scene. The warm night air reminded me of days past.

The aches of the universe seem less impertinent to the young, I romanticise that when I think of the past, all I can do is think about how happy I was. Cool, blush breezes coming in from the sea and our pale bodies sitting on a dark volcanic beach. Beautiful.

Every crack in the pavement reminded me of the slow decay of time. A car sprints by, I have always been here, stuck in limbo. Dancing as I do, around and around the centre point of monotony, the tails of my dress branching out in every direction, looking for signs of life to come and dance with me but there is no one here to dance. The world has stopped moving and soon the music will cease to play and when all the world has stopped and there is no longer any music to hear, then I shall be dumb. As two of my senses leave me then I do expect that the world shall soon turn dark too, perhaps taste shall become bland as I revert to a singularity, unaware of my own existence, imitating the world around me. I wonder if everywhere is just as devoid of humanity. Does the whole world forget how to dance? Perhaps they never heard the music.

Staring at the ground and following my feet, I found that I had arrived at my home. Unmistakably identical to the rest of the row that litters the side of the pavement, I wondered if it was possible for flowers to bloom in these conditions. If they did, I wondered if all of those flowers would look the same. One long row of sickly, yellow, drooping daffodils. I unlocked the door and surveyed the narrow hallway for signs of life.

"That you Lizzie?" Called a familiar voice from down the hall.

I marched down the hallway and found my father sitting in his habitual chair. The middle-aged man looked delighted to see me. His bright brown eyes glistened and a smile grew from what could have only been a forlorn face only a few second earlier. A stained, grey vest drooped across his weak stem, mimicking the pallet of the colour in his face and his sullen cheeks did well to maintain the illusion of peace that he was fighting to maintain. He sat, arched in his high backed, brazenly-dull red chair, looking completely in keeping with the mood of the room and the aroma perpetuating the room was as the earth that feeds it was dying.

"Hey Dad."

As sombre a reply as I tried to give, I couldn't help but entertain his enthusiasm and my response sounded warm. I hate the way he sits in a chair that faces the opening of the living room, away from the sun. It is a pre-emptive cry for attention. It forces anybody who enters to interact with the man and the man always sits in that chair. I pity the man and his lack life-spark, leading him to desperation, it seeps from his every pour. Middle age and in the winter of his life, not through illness but through defeat. I want to pick him up and shake him until the colour returns to his face and the will back to his limbs, scream his name at him until he remembers it. I feel like he is looking for someone to save him and I would if that person was me but it isn't.

"How was the library sweetheart?" He asks, pushing a wavy golden-grey brown lock away from his eyes.

"Oh, you know. It's the library."

I glance up to meet his unwavering gaze and fragile ego at the same time before moving on through the living room, stepping over dead clothes and buried litter to reach the kitchen,

"Or at least I shouldn't lose any sleep over the rapturous, intermittent solace I afforded myself. Is Gael in? I have missed him."

Though I couldn't see him, I could tell the man's heart sunk a little at the prospect of losing the company of his 'little girl', or perhaps that it was that I chose to respond in such a callous and unfiltered manner and no man likes to be shown by a woman that his senses are inferior to his, let alone that of a man twenty two years his junior.

He answers, "Yeah-Sweetheart, he is up in his room..."

I scold myself that I could act so brazen to a man who is not currently of this earth. An apathetic and sullen middle-aged man, his heart swells, it is open but nothing dares come near. I convince myself that I am a wicked and vile woman for having so little thought for one who has spent so much of his time and wasted youth assuring my safety and relative happiness; a man who, in all likelihood, is in his current state because of the darkness that he shielded me from just so that I may have stayed in the light. These days I make my own light though, should I extinguish my own fire just to set his ablaze again? Then perhaps he could do the same for me. We can perpetually reignite each other's souls until one of us dies and leaves the other in darkness. I think this a poor agenda but decide to engage him none the less.

"How is the job hunt going?" I ask, stepping into the room, now clutching a crusty piece of bread.

My father now looks a little taken back by the directness of the question and raises his eyebrows as if being shown a gun, he slowly nods his head, as if only half comprehending the question, "Oh you know how it is Lizzy, a lot people applying to accountancy jobs at the moment. Plus, with the GBH charge, it makes it a little difficult to get an 'in' anywhere you know... but something will come up, real soon, I promise." Dad speaks with the quivering voice of a wounded deer being shown the mantle it is going to spend the rest of its existence on, I can almost see death in his eyes and I can hear his voice shake when he speaks.

"It's ok Dad," I can almost hear a quiver in my voice as well, "You will come through this, I know, you have always been there for me, I couldn't ask for a better father."

Finding a morsel of confidence in himself, he thanks his daughter and smiles at the words, so carefully glittered upon him. "All I need is that bitch-ex wife of mine to give me back my son and I will alright!" He exclaims with the veracity that thinking about his emasculated position in his family bestows on him.

So painfully transparent. My heart anchors further into the dirt to see him so base. So angry. I suspect that he has been drinking but I don't make an accusation. I can't bare the argument. I can't bare the discussion as to why when he has his son but two days of the week, he would let that time spent unceremonious. Gael spends much of his time in his room. Father spends most of his time in his chair. All the while the air gets thinner. A shrivelling sound of silence falls over the room and it seems to get darker. I can hear the clock and it ticks a slow, concise, ravenous tick followed by a contrived, villainous tock, feeding on the elaboration of the monotony of time with the contempt that only one that counts every second could.

I meander upstairs, minding every step as a stepping stone between me and the colours that I have not seen in an age that is too long for my sight. The narrow stairwell is cavernous, seems to grow in stature. My steps seem to disturb agitated frogs that snap at my heels. The top of the stairs is a bog overgrown; laying a brazen testament to a battle that took place some time ago. A battle fought with malice and forked shaped tongues as swords and loneliness for armour. The shields to each soldier's personal battle lay shut in front of me. In the case of my father's, it lay bolted but all had the markings of each of their own personal battles. Dents that lay as constant reminders of times when the swords physically manifested themselves into objects capable of scarring more than just our memories.

Not Gael's door though. Gael's door remained wound-less.

I push open the wooden white flag that separates war from peace and walk across the threshold into a small hovel with glistening red, striped, crystal-ruby red on waxing-cherry crimson wall paper with a bright white and immaculately patterned designed sky above head. The crushing reality of the house and its memories are forgotten. A quaint wardrobe, the sides smoothed so that the most delicate of feathers would nest and feel in their hearts that they were at home. I take care to take in the touch of the soft, plush, grass-like feeling that overwhelms my feet as I enter, I have walked through lush greens in summer that have not felt half as comforting as the ground does feel in that room. The book shelf sits a picture of a thousand colours, ranging from Wells to Orwell, smiling across the room to what was a very small boy, sitting, engulfed, drowning in a light blue bed duvet. The boy sits happily observing one of the missing teeth of his smiling friend, transported far away.

I smile to behold him. His scrawny frame cuddled by a T-shirt befitting a boy twice his size, his bony elbows rest on his knees as his knees are bent towards his chest. His little bony cheeks seem to glow of wisdom beyond that of the years of an eleven year old boy and the deep ridges that encompass his eyes are caves of awe that perceive the world in a curious tone, the way an eager minded young boy should.

"Hey trouble." I speak softly and try to hide all of the joy that I feel upon seeing this small treasure and if I give it all to him now, then I shall have nothing more to give him later. Gael puts his book down immediately; his eyes bounce to mine and his teeth shine enthusiastically.

"Lizz-ee! I have been waiting for you, you said you wouldn't be so late today!" The child tries to scorn me but is incapable holding irksome thoughts.

So, I act wounded, as not to do his feelings disregard. "Oh, forgive me!" and I throw myself across his bed, "Please forgive me sire, the road was long and the journey was arduous."

Gael smiles a smile so bright that Icarus would have flown once more just to get a closer look and have his heart warmed. I remember what it feels like to be alive. Our jovial introductions continued for some time and I bestow upon him many cuddles and many kisses to which he pretends to detest. He jumps over my back and I wrestle him off. I never felt so happy as when I am playing with Gael. At length, Gael stands up and makes his way across his room and pulls out an envelope from a draw containing many secret things that a boy of eleven would treasure. He tries to hide his smile but it is clear to me that he extremely pleased with himself, whatever it is he has put inside the envelope, it is clear it is of great importance to him and he would like it to be of great importance to me too.

"I got this for you!" He pushes the envelope into my hand and stumbles back in an action that looks as much running away as anything.

"What is it?" I ask after him. Gael was fond giving me things, pictures that he has drawn and his writing, amongst other things.

"Open it!" Everything Gael said was said with such excitement. His life pulsated with playful delights; it was all game to him. He couldn't wait to begin having fun when he came into contact with someone he liked. So quiet for a boy his age and so uninterested in society, but he made his own society and filled it with love. Those who he did enjoy the company of, he would hold onto so tightly that they would turn to diamond and feel their time all the more valuably spent as a result.

I open the plain, unmarked envelope and find enclosed in it two tickets to the circus. Though, I was underwhelmed by the idea of attending such an event, the way the boy was looking up at me as I sat on his bed, his wide eyes full to the brim of hope, I knew that it would take just the slightest prick to burst his joy filled bubble. So, without the slightest hint of disappointment or hesitation, I gasped and opened my mouth, meeting his gaze with the same enthusiasm that he was showing me.

"Oh, my Gael, this is wonderful! How did you get these? I hope you didn't spend all your money on them, I would feel ever so guilty. But I love it, I can't wait. You are the most wonderful brother any girl could ask for! You do know how to look after me. One week from now? Won't this be wonderful" The number of superlatives that I did unleash on the poor boy knew no bounds and Gael blushed, unable to contain the sense of pride and adulation that he had brought upon himself and I.

"I just got them!" He blurted out.

"Well, I can't wait to go, you cheeky little money," and I smiled at him, then we hugged a long embrace, I thought of the weight of life and responsibilities to other human beings within society.

 The obligations of human interaction. An utterly unprofitable acquisition, when looked at from any direction. Yet, all encompassing, the centre of what it is to be human. Tearing as apart from the outside in, questioning what is right and what is wrong and what is even real. What it is to be alive is a surreal course of interactions, knocking us from one path to another, until we are quite sure we are lost, but if the smiling faces that are on that path look familiar and fill us with joy, then we are truly never lost. Nothing is ever really forgotten. It lives on, inside of us, forever. What has happened is just as relevant now as it was when it happened. In this throwaway society, we treat the people around us and our acquaintances as trowels. The trowel digs a hole in the earth to which we hope that flowers will grow. An impersonal tool. Treat the tools to which you hope to dig your flowers with well. I shall be the eternal gardener and plant flowers forever.

Elizabeth and Gael in the Woods

A small beetle is making its casual way just beyond my foot. It is round; a shiny blue. I wonder if beetles are capable of empathy. I put myself in the shoes of a beetle but seem to fall a little short because I am incapable of shrinking myself so that thought becomes singular and easily led.

I reach for a small, lazy branch and give it its orders to make acquaintance with the beetle, the beetle obliges as if it were a passenger stepping onto a train.

There lies the difficulty of empathising with a beetle, if a phantom train arrives at a station, I would at least pause to think about where it is going and think of my own personal safety in stepping on board such an enigmatic and illustrious carriage. But the beetle does it as if it were what it was destined to do its whole life.

"It walks like it is in a dream", Gael puzzles next to me.

"In dreams we don't wonder where we are going…", I fit the pieces together. Perhaps nature is dreaming as it pours its self into the world, time being but a vile to fill and a veil to stay forever masked. Maybe that is why I struggle to empathise with a beetle, the beetle is dreaming and I am awake.. What an egotistical, closed minded and above all human notion. 'I am more awake than nature, more conscious' The nature that has been here long before I was burdening the grass; the nature that will be here long after death has decided to stop watching me and finally come over and make his acquaintance.

"Lizzy?", The upward inflection lets me know that he wants me to do him a favour.

"No", I raise my chin and cross my arms as if impersonating a grumpy child.

"Oh pleaseeeeee", the other one persists.

"Nope."

"But you don't even know what I want yet."

"Okay, you win, what do you want, the world? I'll give you the world Gael, or the sky, how about the sky Gael? Perhaps I shall steal up to Atlas as he sleeps, tickle him under his arm and then steal the sky, how about that Gael, would you like the sky?"

Gael opened his mouth to say something then paused.

"I think the sky would be heavy, I'll let you keep it."

"Thank you, Gael, you have left me with the sky, you think I want to hold it up? I am happy that the sky is there, but I don't want to be responsible for it, you have doomed me. This is why I call you trouble."

"No, Lizzy, I just want to climb that tree", he points to a willow tree across the park, golden, glistening, catching the sun's rays and seeming to hold them, savouring them in its grandeur countenance.

"Then go and climb the tree! You little money", I reply with a false indignance.

"With you", Gael adds, with a wonder struck smile but he knows I don't climb trees.

"Your faith in me is admirable but very badly misplaced Gael."

"Well, can you come and watch?"

There is something immeasurably powerful and distinct about the trees in summer. During the winter months I tend to gloss over trees. Their forlorn faces reek of death, as if all of the skin has been flayed from them, they are the living carcass of that which was and is so sporadically alive. Here, in the air, in the trees, death has decided to let beauty be. Or perhaps death changes with the season, for death must be master of the fate of more than people, but of woodland animals, insects and trees too. I wonder if death is fonder of trees and that is why he lets them live for so long. A tree's offspring and social circle seem to die and be reborn as quickly, perhaps death appreciates the business, or doesn't and a trees extraordinary life is a punishment for giving the beady eyed stalker so much work to do. Such a burden, the life of a human, so much death. To live ten more times over, to witness death's work, over and over. Does a tree become desensitised to the dark, flowing, abrasive and sudden ends? Perhaps it is why the trees do not talk.

"A quoi bon dire", I whisper to myself. The trees must feel like there is no point in talking, death will have the final word anyway. A breeze hits me; shivers my spine.

A tree in the summer is much more to behold though. Its skin looks radiant, glowing, pouring out with soft, defiant waves of colour. It seems to get warmer the closer we approach it. If death's effect on trees in the winter is that of stricken depravity, then death must be born again this summer. His skin is soft, plush. The beady, dark eyes are become the wells of hope that embody the bountiful wealth of youth and gaiety. The icy stare of barren and forsaken justice is nothing more than a careful glance and a warm smile of an eternally mature man that wants youth to frolic in being young. After all, what could ever really die, that has never really lived.

"I need a boost Lizzy," Gael's eyes never leave the tree. How can he be so sure of himself? It is as if the little acorn knows exactly what he wants.

"Just don't fall," My voice has become sullen. I give Gael his boost and watch him take the first branch. He hoists himself up, effortlessly. I am surprised by his vigour.

I find it difficult to comprehend the fearless nature of children. As Gael takes branch after branch, climbing higher and higher he puts a higher and higher stake on his activity. What puzzles me is why he would put up such a high stake, he must be all in now, with nothing to win. Perhaps he just enjoys playing. Perhaps the method is the most important thing to him.

Is this something ingrained in just Gael and children and people like Gael? Or is this something that people have in them but then lose as time grows sterner. I should love to live as one who is obsessed with the process and not the outcome. I should love that my life could be purposeless and beautiful…

"How far are you going to climb Gael?" I call up, he has already climbed higher than I thought was safe but I don't want to stifle him, fill his mind with doubt, especially not at this point.

"I am going to climb until I can no longer reach the next branch!" He calls after. Then he pauses for a second and follows up, "and when I can longer reach the next branch, I shall come down and wait until I grow, I shall climb the tree and then reach the next branch!"

I try to resist the urge but I could not stop myself, "What will happen when you reach the top?" I release this narcissistic length of scaly dark rope into Gael's green and blue world without any kind of leash, any kind of guise. It is unkind to introduce forethought to such a beautiful method. I think I did it because I was jealous. I saw Gael sparkling and I could bare to feel so filthy beneath him, I feel shame. If Gael decides that he has a purpose, then what he is doing will cease to be beautiful. What he is doing would cease to be an action but a method and a method, a method is something that cruel men have, an agenda. When I consider a conversation, I think of all of the people who have an agenda. A teacher trying to 'help'; a priest trying to gain power, a boy led by lust, a quest for knowledge, for the sake of appearances. What if we could meet a stranger and talk without pretence, without seeking to gain the upper hand, without sub plotted mind games, intuition and second guessing. If words could just be exchanged between two people, there would be no 'reaching the top', just climbing, no one would care which branch they are sitting on either or how high up they are, who is above or below them, because there would be no motive to care. A child is not motivated to climb a tree, nor should he need to be. I wish that I could take back the words but they have already been said. I sparked fire that might destroy a white piece of paper. No sooner said did the words taste bitter on my lips. I wait fearfully and anxiously. I created the thunder that I fear.

Gael pauses for a second, he looks like he is searching inside himself for an answer that he doesn't have, then suddenly, the answer seems obvious to him,

"I shall look from the top for another tree to climb!" The words fall light upon my heart and I breathe a sigh of relief for the impending grief that threatened to take Gael from a path covered in leaves leading nowhere and simultaneously everywhere to a very straight and narrow path. No one knows where that first path leads but the second leads to death. The death of all things, both physical and metaphysical. Death of emotion, of hope. The moment you have a purpose is the moment you become an island, and a machine.

"Oh no, not today, it shall be dark before long. I shall never find you and you will have to live in the trees, forever!" The joy and whimsy return to my voice, the warmth to my heart.

"No Lizzy, I don't want to live in a tree!" Gael calls as he unholsters one leg to start climbing down.

"Are you sure?"

"I am positive that I never want to live in a tree"

"One day you might have to…"

But Gael didn't hear me.

Perhaps it is just women that nature thrusts purpose upon.

If I can't climb my tree without a purpose or at least with someone who wants nothing from me, then I would rather climb my tree alone. Perhaps if faced with such a decision I would choose not to climb a tree at all.

An Exercise in Saying Nothing

"The roses in Patricia's hair look lovely. It is though the far-removed blossoms of summer have come once more, smiling. It is a triumph of he will over nature. A bold statement."

Rachael gazes imperially over at Patricia, her eyes seem to dance languidly with a few ideas before-

"I think that you are too generous. Or, I think that this is the first time I have ever heard you say anything nice about old Pat," her voice trails off, provincially, throwing the final words out of her world and telling them not to look at her, they can keep the change. But they do look at her. And so do I.

"Now I am sure that simply cannot be t-"

"You think that old Pat is ugly, stumpy and fat, so you complimented the things that is furthest removed from her," her eyes are cold and distracted as she fumbles for a cigarette.

"I most certainly do not."

"I think that when you compliment people for the superficial effort that you put in that you sound fake."

It is true; Patricia is ugly. No rose, nor any flower picked from anyone's Edan could change that. But I persist the for the sake of saving my face.

"She may not be the most gifted of creation but the roses are a marked improvement."

"I guess it detracts from her form and that is a blessing for all… I have never understood the fascination with roses… I understand that joyful women enjoy being surrounded by colourful flowers to hide and distract from how plain and dirty they feel… Blood-red often. Spitefully spikey. Prudent, they die without the comfort of others; they are incapable of living in this world by themselves. They have become domesticated. Perhaps, once, wild roses would have been a defiant triumph against nature. Rising, clouted in blood, armed to the teeth. Death-marred colour, swirling, engulfing. Roses are pampered, devoid of independence. So, perhaps that is what you mean? "Patricia looks delightfully domesticated-" Said Elizabeth," Rachael looks like she has begun to run, gears turning.

I protest, but to avail.

She continues, "I assure you that the flowers that you read about long ago are very different o the flowers here. I am sure that if you looked a little closer, you might see that what you thought was magic, or a promise, actually looks a lot more like a weed, caped in cheap perfume. Your mind's eye plays tricks on you."

It is difficult to adhere to a theory that paints you to be a daemon.

"Pat you beautiful woman come here," Rachael beckons Patricia, subordinate-Patricia obeys. "Pat, how are you today my little rose cake? Did you end up watching Hollyoaks the other night?"

Rachael does not watch Hollyoaks.

"Well yahhh, it was a Wednesday night wasn't it?" Patricia's face lights up like a Christmas tree. Flashing florescent lights blinding her eyes, so one could not see the tapering of her soul. "It was like I was telling Tommy, I could not believe that Tim was just a voice inside that woman's head and that woman's little brother got caught with the snakes…"

"By far my favourite character, I simply could not live without him, I was sad to see things happen like that…" Rachael fakes her way through a conversation before fluttering away to some other corner of civility. Living inside the glowing embers of other people's newly roaring light.

Everyone puts themselves at the centre of their own universe.

"So, you must be Elizabeth," Patricia's demeanour is, unremarkably, more reserved.

"So I must be, I like the roses in your hair, Patricia isn't it…" and a more amiable conversation was never had, but it wasn't particularly interesting.

Then a young man walked over, it was Patricia's brother and she insisted on introducing me to him.

"I think you should meet my brother," my objections had no effect, before I knew what was happening. "Elizabeth, meet Mr. Darcy."

I think that joke may have been the entire reason she is doing this. The man, who has clearly been dragged against his will, looks to his sister will impatient unwilling eyes, with contempt. However, he checks himself for long enough to shake my hand.

"It is a pleasure."

"Like wise," he is not a handsome man, at least not in the traditional sense of grooming but he is unkempt, and broad.

"It's not really Darcy, is it?" I ask the man.

"No, it is Michael, I shall never have any idea why my sister insists on introducing me to people this way." The tall, shaggy man shoots his sister an obstinate, hateful glance, devoid of all affection. They are most certainly siblings.

Patricia looks flustered now, looking about her for help, "I think I just heard one of the girls talking about me, I am going to go and sort her out," The clumsy woman leaves in a hurry, glowing.

It is clear that we both understand Patricia's 'subtle as the opening of the gates of hell' approach to match making and I think that he is more mortified than I. This tremendously insulting. His dirty locks hang over his eyes for a moment as he visibly grits his teeth before unclenching them and accepting his position. I look away, slightly embarrassed, before eventually mustering smile to give to him and I look back up. Despite my uncomfortable position, it would be terribly unfeminine of me to begin the conversation, I should adhere to the rules of engagement and give him a chance to assert some masculinity.

But he doesn't. He keeps his head bowed, doing everything to avoid eye contact, though accidentally making it through side long glances and completely ignoring conversation all together. His broad figure remains stern; it is the torso of a proud statue. Time went on like this, uncomfortably, I was becoming quite self-conscious and embarrassed. The silence between us had become so great that I became conscious of my breathing as it seemed so loud to me. My hand felt warm and my heart grew dim and distressed. My mind races and I ponder what could make a man so rude, to be so stern and reserved in his own countenance to ignore and by the same mark, insult his company, thrust upon him or not. It crosses my mind that perhaps this isn't a man at all but a frightened little boy, too fragile and overcome by a social situation to continue.

So I try to help him, "The weather is nice," I say indifferently, looking far away as I do, as to give some auspicious sign that a conversation wouldn't be refuted.

Clear, concise, without stutter or nervous impediment, "I can't say that I take delight in this kind of weather, the plane and easy sun is a passenger on trivial conversation, often made by about the sun itself. Rain, I prefer immeasurably to the sun.

"Oh," I make my abrupt reply to such a disagreeable sentiment and return to unusual silence.

However, not a great deal of it was allowed to pass, as no sooner had I been insulted that the man, bold as a rock, prepares himself for his departure.

"It has been a pleasure to meet you," Flashing his eyes to meet my ghostly gaze, briefly before looking away, "I am afraid I am pre-engaged."

As abruptly as he appeared, he was gone. I briefly pause and muse over who he might be meeting. It occurs to me that he could be leaving me and being so rude to me because he has another woman to see. Perhaps he would do her the courtesy of participating in a conversation. However, I decide that I am satisfied to have lost the company of a misguided and impertinent young boy.

The garden perpetuates its feelings of hopeful, youthful vigour and anxious introductions. I can feel its heartbeat, it swells. Beats faster with every new introduction. I look around myself to find many youthful exchanges of pleasantries. Young men with youthful haircuts and too much testosterone trying to be introduced to young women with colourful clothing. It looks like a fun game.

The man makes his over to a small group of girls, the less the better and if you can find a suitable target on her own then that is even better, however it is still early in the evening so this young buck has to work with what he has and approaches a group of four women. He does his best to look confident, trying to smile and look at the women as he approaches, made possible by the elevation of his blood alcohol level, he walks confidently and purposefully over to where the females gather.

"I don't know many people here; do you mind if I stay with you until I find someone I know?" "I was just standing over there and couldn't help but overhear your conversation" "Heaven must be missing an angel…" Or something of the effect, I can't actually hear his conversation, one of the above.

This particular male, shoulders broad, slim, chin pointed in the right direction, slicked back, blonde hair- a little shaved at the side, because he is 'edgy', just like a child wearing a red and black dragon shirt to a school disco. This young specimen acts like he has fortune wrapped around his fingertips. However, it is not his finger tips that I am focusing on but his eyes and they are beginning to shake. They shake from one woman to another because he didn't think he would get this far and hasn't properly identified his target, at this point he is in open water without a paddle and a large shadow is beginning to form under his boat. He looks desperately from one woman to another and they look about ready to stone him. Desolate, desperate looks. You can feel his eyes crawling over every inch of these women. Starting at the grass, because the grass that one stands upon is as important a part of a person as their fingers or their gloves. Where a person stands, is their position in the universe at that particular point in time and every decision they have ever made has led them to be in that spot. His eyes fumble over the women's flats and heels alike. Faster. He inhales in apprehension as he looks over their legs and skirts. He scurries over their breasts as though he barely knew what they were and certainly doesn't recognise them or admit to any kind of affection towards such base objects… A desperate and poor adventure. Most of his time is spent trying not to look at the floor. Poor young boy; banging his head against a wall. Trying to do the things to prove that he is not so small. He looks as though he is going to cry. The women look as though they are enjoying themselves though. This is entertainment. The prettier, more experienced of the women make constant eye contact. They are trying to intimidate and immaculate the young buck, for dominance is the only real class system. Jack (I like Jack) seems like he is desperate to get to the top of this hill, even though it would appear that he is falling down. Most of these hunts end in failure. However, it would appear that a Jill has fallen down too because as the other women make to leave, Jill (a very plain and slightly over fed flower) has decided to take root in Jack's garden. The other, more experienced and prettier women knew better and left the situation having elevated their status. However, the less experienced, duller specimen knows no better. Two people with no self-respect take it upon themselves to dilute the gene pool.

Meandering, as I am, a ghost sitting on a log, floating down the stream. I walk through people but find myself catching the eye of everyone I pass. Perhaps it is paranoia. My disposition is becoming a little flustered. I check myself, brush myself down and even check my mirror, quaintly hidden in my pocket. The same eyes stare back; not that I recognise them. I haven't recognised them in some time. When I see a pair of eyes, I find it difficult to distinguish them from my own. Each pair of eyes peers out from a deep cove. In this little cove is some little piece of magic, sparking reason and deciphering! Taking input, consciousness. To be conscious is a mystery to me. It is difficult to tell the difference in one person's consciousness and another's. I know that my consciousness is different from a cat's because of how we communicate… I can't see it; I can only experience my own and I don't believe that I experience consciousness the same way as any other human beings… At least I hope not, or otherwise, what is the point of there being more than one person in existence. My eyes, my body, they could belong to anyone. I struggle to recognise myself beyond my thoughts. The entire experience makes it difficult to be at a party. I don't feel like in these short conversations that I can get to know anyones thoughts or the spark beyond those thoughts. Perhaps that is what parties are meant for: a taster, to see if individuals like each other and want to get to know each other better in the future. Throwaway society… I don't believe that I see these people as anything more than half shattered visages of how they would like to be seen. Perhaps my filter is broken.

"Elizabeth!" a voice calls warmly to me. It is nice to see Rachael's eyes again, though they are not as warm as her voice, not as endeared to me and when earlier, each glance seemed to communicate a thousand words, now I am receiving the whispers of a conversation long since lost. I, slowly, hesitantly walk over to where she resides, she is caught in solemn but purposeful conversation with two women two whom it is clear that Rachael considers to be of great consequence, or at least that is the impression she is giving. Rachael looks engrossed with what the woman has to say, gives them all of the attention that one might give a coiled snake or perhaps a scorpion with its tail held high. I must be some kind of sleeping caterpillar to these or at least in context of the conversation, as Racheal maintains all of the eye contact with her former company. These women are as water with one another.

"I hope you have finished entreating that young boy Miss Elizabeth," Rachael says coolly, the girls look at each other and collectively they seem to sparkle. The remark brings me back from some other part of the world that I had drifted off to.

"I assure you, I have absolutely no idea what you mean," my choice of words are amiable enough. However, it is easy to observe the reluctant nature of the words, how they are said. One word seems to hang or and get caught on another, like people caught out in open water for the first time, these words are lost, panic, frolic and cling on to one another in a desperate attempt to stay buoyant, but as each words it's the floor, the sounds become disfigured, the shapes become deformed. I carry on, "That is to say, that the man is quite rude and I assure you, I have already forgotten his name," now I feel myself blushing for nothing more than the openness of having such a personal conversation with strangers.

"She likes him," one of the girls jostles loose in movement borne most likely of jealously and directed towards position and power.

I deny this as it is not true; I feel embarrassed at the conversation though. I am a little upset with the the accusation. I should not be caught again with a man so impertinent. I don't want to be mixed with dirty paint. It is not so hard to see that I am a water colour and that my colours of liable to run. To fall in love… I should become all at once mixed up when I decide to fall in love. Our colours shall run together in a vigorous and elegant shade that I will have never seen before. To be mixed up with this stern, obnoxious character should darken my shade, he is a black or worse, a grey. If he should be a purple, then I scarcely dread to think of the abomination that I should become. What should I become when my colours begin to run. Perhaps I should bleed so much colour that it begins to run dry and I become a shaking-shell, old and withered. Where does that colour go? With those younger than me, of that I have doubt as it seems that the less colour I can find in myself, the more vibrant the pool gets. What should happen if I fall in love with someone who is not a painting? Perhaps I should fall in love with a harsh man: tactless; colourless. Spends his time in matters of 'great consequence', a business man, a man who sacrifices is time and his life for material gain. Cladding himself in sparkling, multi coloured robes. But these robes will always appear colourless, invisible. We with the colour on the inside will always know that those that feel the need to clad themselves in rainbows are boring.

"Where do you go lizzie?"

"Fallen down a rabbit hole," Earnestly, I am not sure who was speaking to me, it sounded like something that I may have said about myself.

None the less, I feel obligated to reply as all three women are staring at me at this point, waiting for a reply.

"I didn't fall, I jumped." Rachael, who I am standing closest with, did not seem like she could contain her elation within her wicked and wry smile. The other women looked grave and feel deadly quiet.

Clowns and Knives

A low rumble of murmuring, jittering paroxysms of adulation and unbridled satisfaction began to force itself on us as I and Gael gazed, wide eyed, engaged in a stoic transient.

"I'm really excited." Gael forced out; he glanced sideways in a naive effort to conceal his reservations.

The nearer we drew, the more the ambient, ghoulish-glow rose, like a spectre. The red misted lights seemed to glow avariciously and intensify as a newly made wound would bleed a little at first and then profusely. New wounds were conjured, one after the other and strobe lights struck as lightning in to the air. An artificial thunder rose as goliath, leering over the top of our horizon with eyes screaming a dominating roar that loomed more impressive the closer we drew.

"Me too monkey!" I looked down and made strong eye contact with Gael and smiled assuredly.

Thumping hammered through the ether as the air became denser and more powerful; it seemed to electrify the counted seconds the closer we drew. What started off as a low murmur was now beginning to grab at my heart, forcing its self upon me as dreams protruding in darkness wrap its arms around my neck to pull me closer and show me it's teeth. A chorus of coordinated screams seemed to rise on cue and die as the music would build confidence and stature, before coming down to vanquish sanity in a violent attack.

The closer we got; the whiter Gael looked. Presently, clambering, grasping for my hand, Gael took hold for support but held himself tall although rigid. I squeezed his hand and bent down in front of him. The monster fresh from out of the closet was looming down over my shoulders. "You don't have to go any further Gael; we can go home. Get back on the bus we came on and forget that we ever came here.

"No, I want to go!" Gael's voice squeaked with something caught in his throat.

"It's okay Gael, we can go home, you're terrified, why do you want to go on?" I pursued.

"I got you a present Lizzie and I want you to have fun, everyone always says that you never have any fun, well tonight you are going to let something loose..." Gael trailed off as he realised that he didn't know what I was supposed to let loose. It dawned upon me that these weren't his words.

"Did someone put you up to this Gael?" I asked with, curious and stern, "Who bought these tickets Gael?"

The questioning had made Gael inconsolable, he quivered with torment from outside and in. His big glistening eyes looked out from their stony coves as he gathered one moment of passion and resolve.

I made to leave, "Come on Gael, lets g-"

"Noooo!" Gael screeched, retreating his hand, "I-got the tickets," now breathing heavily, "It's- my- rrrrsponsbility- for you to have a good time." With that, Gael flew. I was so shocked by the uncharacteristic outburst that I didn't make for him until after he had rasped past.

Into the open jaws of the static night, he ran like Pheidippides, possessed with burdens of adulthood eating at a growing soul too small to be encumbered with freights of failure. Towards the rising curtain of night lights and earthquakes I followed with the swiftness of a lioness as in that moment I could perceive that Gael was more afraid of letting me down than he was of charging head first into the seven armies of hell.

Headlong he crashed into their front-line battlements and was lost, swept under a sea of jubilant demons. They remonstrated with each other, moving like a hive of delirious hive-minded insects and Gael was to contest in their depths.

I chased, spirited by fear and anguish.

An ambassador of Mars was sent to welcome me with crossed arms of malignant malice. Tremendous, the iron figure standing tall and proud, dashed in colour of bright, brutal flowing vermillion, drooling yellow, fragmentations of green hissed in spots. Smiling manically, his rosy red cheeks seemed to glow with anticipation and his patched overalls were adorning to banner degradation. He looks over his loyal minions, surveying and entreating the dogs of war and orchestrating degeneration.

The scene was not at all as I had expected. Where I had expected juggling acts stood carnival stalls, occupied with villains missing teeth and decorum. I might have feigned to see glitter, streamers and colour pertaining to jovial acts of elation. I was confronted with bars, congregated as waterholes, large alpha males sought attention from dominant females in poorly written but timelessly rehearsed acts. Males feign dominance as a female hierarchy is contested; only those playing the game even know that the game is being played. Maroon cups were used to serve alcohol. The calm, timid, genial playground-music was replaced with several different DJ ensembles, performing different medleys of songs that I had never heard the like of up to that night. Triumphantly, rising through the middle, Everest, a red and white big top. It was so large that the rest of the events that unfolded beneath it seems to happen to insects. Commanding jovial and eccentric demur, Women, wearing short blouses and shorter shorts, clouted in colour clamoured to attention.

"Smack that, give me some more" I had heard this song before, but I had no idea that it existed in any other capacity than in the world of fiction, I didn't know that such coarse sexual exploitation could adhered to.

I watched a young woman, who couldn't have been much older than twenty, though it is difficult to tell with through war paint. Tall, black hair sleeking no further than shoulder length. Her clothes were tight and fitted impressively to her figure. She wasn't doing anything beyond being a socialite. However, the manner in which she achieved it caused her to be the envy of all that surrounded her. Floating, like an apparition of hedonism and overwhelming mortal desire the clouds parted as she walked. She had power. I couldn't take my eyes away. This was a grandeur of self-empowerment or a desperate cry for attention. A call for sibilance or a cry for individualism. She was crossed and met by the gaze of hypnotised men and contemptuous women.

I moved on through the hysteria until at last I found Gael, sitting on the lap of a middle-aged gentleman dressed in black, thin loose-fitting clothes that seemed to fall off him as he sat calmly. His strewn, lied back hair clung to his scrawny figure and his bony features protruded from his gently grinning face. I rushed to Gael and put my arms around him, expecting him to fall apart into my arms but to my surprise, he had calmed down considerably since his earlier impertinence. I scolded him and told him never to rush of from me again and assure him that we should be going straight home.

"Don't worry Lizzy, I have been talking to Mr. Savage, he is a DJ here and has been very wonderful, haven't you Mr. Savage?" Gael looked up at the gentleman as pulled Gael down from his lap and to my side.

The man stood up straight, he looked taller than he did sitting down, pulled his clothes around him and started in a reserved, kind and welcoming demeanour, "I am very sorry if I have been of any inconvenience ma'am, I was simply consoling young Gael here, he seemed ever so upset"

Gael replied for me, "Mr. Savage is in the circus! And is a very nice man."

I remonstrated with Gael and Mr. Savage for a little while and indeed the gentleman was a DJ with the circus and explained that a lot of people get confused and arrive expected a different kind of show to the one on offer.

"You simply must stay to watch my show though," continued Mr. Savage, "after all the ordeal that has taken place so far, I fear the worst of it is over and it should be a shame if you were leave without the pleasure."

"Can we stay? Please Lizzy, stay and listen to the music," Gael insisted.

"Here is some passes to get you into the VIP area, it is much quieter and I can keep an eye on you both there," he put the cards around our necks, "come find me in my office after the show, I feel we would have much to talk about, like your countenance and I have a son Gael's age that is always complaining that he doesn't have anyone to play with, please come and keep us company after the show? I wish I could stay and here your answer, but I must get ready for the show, I am on in no time at all. The main stage, come watch"

I wasn't sure what to make of it, but Gael has always been such a terrific judge of character.

With Gael being a little calmer than before we persisted in trying to enjoy our time at the carnival. Despite earlier assumptions the entire countenance of the hive of activity was one of good-natured fun looking at through a new tint. The snarling, rough and rugged men seemed nothing more than smiling naughty children, intent on making sure the guests of the carnival were kept in jovial, raucous spirits.

"Three throws for a pound darlin'," one called out. The ugly puzzle of his dialect even seemed charming and I was almost flattered and most certainly charmed by the impertinence of his temperament.

"How about it Gael? Would you like to have a go at knocking the bottles over?" Gael had retreated back into himself as would be expected of such a highly social event but reluctantly agreed.

"Awe, not this time Gael, better luck next time," I upheld in good spirits.

"One more go, one more go, I think I can win this time!" Gael insisted, jostling with enthusiasm.

I consented, justifying that his growing confidence was worth paying for.

I turned to the side and happened to glance upon the young socialite girl playing in the stall next to us, she didn't seem to be very good, throwing her balls well wide as she remarked exhaustingly,

"By lord and heaven, I can't hit anything tonight!" She was much better spoken than I even could have given her credit for and seemed to be a perfect juxtaposition her surroundings.

"I think these games are fixed," I said to her, much without thinking, I suppose my earlier time watching her felt like a line of sibilance. She gave me half of her attention and used it to smile disarmingly as she glanced to the floor and then took aim again.

"I dare say a child would have more success than me." She joked.

"Not from what I have seen," I mocked of Gael, smirking in his direction as he knocked the very top bottle off.

"Hey! Don't talk about me like I'm not here!" Gael said with high spirits as he prepared to line up his next three balls.

The girl and I laughed and looked about each other.

"You don't come out a great deal so you?" the girl wondered meeting my countenance with her own.

To which I enquired, "How can you tell?"

"Well, you are not dressed the same way as the rest of the girls here. The jumper and glasses are a give-away. Most of the girls here wear what it is that will stand out the most, which is ironic because all they have achieved is the subtle art of blending in. You on the other hand have worn the most inconspicuous dressage that you could have and yet you stick out like blood spilling over a porcelain sink. I'm Rachael"

The simile that she used troubled me and made me curious of how many times she had seen an image of that nature. It was a relief to meet the acquaintance of a relatively normal person that I share my discomfort with.

"My name is Elizabeth, are you going to be watching Mr. Savage this evening?"

"DJ Savage? Yes, it is who I came to see"

"Well, myself and my little brother just happened to procure a couple of VIP passes, if you are quite alone this evening, as we are, I would be assiduously grateful for your company in a crowd of strangers"

"That is very kind of you, I think I should accept"

....
....
....

The show was a great success, Gael and myself and Rachael had a wonderful time, my only regret being that with all the loud music that I didn't have a chance to really talk and get to know my new friend. Rachael insisted that she had somewhere to be not long before the end of the show, so we swapped numbers and assured each other that we would meet up and she would repay my kindness to which I agreed. Gael and I went in search of Mr. Savage who had insisted on seeing us again before the evening was over.

"Elizabeth! I didn't think that I would get to see you again, come in and know me better my child," He smiled an inviting smile; spoke softly and gaily. "Welcome back Gael, I trust that you enjoyed the show."

"Very much so sir, when the 'beat dropped',"(Gael insisted on knowing the correct terminology in order to converse properly with Mr. Savage) "I couldn't help but close my eyes and dance and when I opened them again, I noticed everyone was doing the same! I was so excited! Tell me, when can I come again?" Gael could not contain his excitement, it would seem at that moment the earth revolved around Mr. Savage and Gael had found his new hero.

Mr. Savage turned to me with a wry half smile "He is an excitable one, isn't he?" Then leaning over and talking, much more jovially to Gael, "How about next time the circus is town? Gael, my son is in the next room, he is just as excited about the show as you are but the poor boy has no one to talk to, would you be my hero and keep him company for a while, I'm sure he will find you terribly interesting."

Gael scampered off into the next room to find his play mate, jubilant at the prospect of making Mr. Savage happy and finding someone to share his joy with. It wasn't long before the two of them were listening to the same music that they had just heard and no doubt dancing in the same manner as the concert.

Mr. Savage turned to me, his brow sweaty, his demeanour was much looser than it was before, and he seemed to sway a little as if being in time with a song that only he could hear. As if coming back to reality, he gestured towards a table and chairs.

"Here, please, sit down- make yourself comfortable, you must be exhausted after the show," he exclaimed in gentle tone.

It was true, I was exhausted, my calves ached from chasing after Gael earlier and my feet were throbbing, i was only too eager to sit down, in fact, if I hadn't a seat to sit in a probably would have sat on the floor.

He proceeded, "Tell me Elizabeth, have you ever seen trees so green, that emeralds would weep in jealousy, fields so gentle that dormice should seem giants of industry in amongst its blades?"

"I'm not sure to what it is you are referring to sir, I have seen a great many things that are both vibrant and delicate, paintings by Picasso, symphonies by Mozart-" I started.

"Of course, you have, you have the eyes of a child. This whole world must seem like a theme park ride to you, twisting and turning, every pivot a new sensation and every piece of it's steely structure a pillar in which God could lay," Mr Savage's eyes were wide; he was excited, "Here," He promptly produced two glasses followed by a bottle that he deemed vodka, "You simply must have a drink with me," the devil was in him now.

"I don't think so sir, I hardly ever drink, and I think you would find me a very poor partner," I replied in earnest.

Mr. Savage was not deterred, "You simply must have one drink with me, to celebrate! Come now, after the show that I put on for you, it would be rude to deny me this most base of requests."

Reluctantly I accepted to one drink. He poured them out, we toasted, to a good show and to a good night, then he threw his to the back of his throat and swallowed; he then implored me to do them same. I almost gagged, screwing up my face at the taste. I was disgusted.

"That was simply awful, what on earth was that?" I am not sure what I was thinking.

"You don't need to worry about that, pretty bird" Mr. Savage seemed to grow in stature, though still sitting in his seat, he breathes more heavily, i could almost see the blood coursing through his veins.

"I think I am going to leave," I said finally.

No sooner had I said these words though was Mr Savage upon me. With his right hand, he covered my mouth so that I couldn't scream, I struggled and tried to resist, but was rendered frozen when with his left hand he produced a large serrated knife.

"There is one thing that we have to get very clear, right here and right now. You have no power any more, you pretty, little bird. All your fancy words and your fancy demeanour with your under dressed clothes and 'I am more poncy than thou' attitude, it's gone because I say it's gone. What I also want you to understand is the size of this blade that I so raggedly hold to your neck, "He flashed the blade in front of my eyes and his eyes flashed with it, "If you so much as speak a word, I will stick this thing into the side of your neck, it will break the bloody vessels in your neck, blood will course down your throat and you couldn't scream if you wanted to. You are not screaming, one way or another, do you understand me?" his voice was meaner, more common, he seemed so angry and so powerful.

He took his hand away from my lips, grabbed the top of my T-shirt, pulled me unto him and kissed me. I shook, terrified. I could feel his tongue as I grimaced, a serpent, attacking something gentle. He removed his lips and replaced it with his hand again.

"I know what you're thinking, I will never get away with this, someone will help you! But guess what? They won't. Nobody is going to disturb us, and nobody is going to believe you if you tell anybody what has happened. And I will tell you why, because you are drunk, you are a stupid, rough drunk girl who wanted to get it on with a DJ at a concert. No one believe you if you told them what had happened. So, if I were you, I would accept your fate and march forth into the open arms of hell like a good little girl" He is nodding now, a little more relaxed, calm, like he is the calm before the storm. He starts his knife down at the bottom of my shirt. I am Shaken and a couple of tears are jogged loose. He cuts, snatches and tears my shirt open. I cling to the chair, backed into a corner, unable to move. My wings are broken. He starts up kissing me again, he slaps me. I grimace, he kisses me again, he slaps me vigorously again. He grabs me by the neck and holds the knife to my head. he is putting so much pressure on my windpipe that I can breathe. I am prey.

"Okay birdy, now you are going to close your eyes and you are going suck anything that comes into your mouth."

He slowly begins to unbutton his jeans, maintaining eye contact with me as he does so. I am weeping uncontrollably. My mind fills and swells with the thousands of leagues of dark sea, light is bereft from my eyes.

It was at that moment that I happened to chance at a figure beyond my tormentor's shoulders. A small figure. It grew larger and all at once was upon Mr. Savage! Concerned, He reacted with lustrous fury, he was possessed, taken like a lunatic, writhing. A low groan erupted from him, growing louder and more unkempt until it reached a shriek. Struggling like a rat caught in a trap. As he whirled, his knife flashed. I helped myself to my feet to find Gael- huddled, like a new born baby. The blood from his chest, bleeding a little at first but then a lot. Mr Savage's son gawped from the doorway. Mr Savage stood, motionless and shell shocked over the heavy fragile figure sprawled on the floor/ Gael made very little noise but clutched his chest.

"Mummy, I want my Mummy." Gael's tender voice was glass.

Dream in the Forest

I am constantly reliving my dreams…

A voluptuous carpet of thorny weeds is interwoven and working together to form some sort of path in amongst the rabble of overgrown life, skittered and scattered across the floor. A canopy of leaves blocks my view but small rays of light trickle down through the growth. The rays are defiant, death shakes his bowed, forlorn head and sets to work, as he does at the foot of hospital beds.

I stand side by side with a man I know only as my partner, my lover before we stroll through the forest. Twists and turns and lying all about our feet, it as if a great many people have taken a great many paths, or perhaps just one person has taken many paths. In any case we saunter down the well-trodden path.

Like a clumsy sprite, she comes bustling and tumbling through the trees. "What do you see? What do you see?" This mad apparition, frantic and agitated, is wearing the baggy clothes of a parlour made of the Victorian era. An off colour, stained apron hangs about her waist and a puffy old bonnet sits on her head.

"What do you see?"

I decline to answer.

"What do you see?" The hysterical woman, half drowned in her own panic, persists. Her manic screams penetrate the air. Her hair is so brown and does nothing to captivate the down of her. Frightened eyes, drenched in fear. She moves her lips, but I do not hear.

"What do you see?!" She asks a final time. I decline to answer as I know that I am wrong. I do not see what she sees.

She scampers off into the over growth, as quickly as her prudent entrance.

It is just now, that we are all alone, that I can hear voices… Not just one but two. I hear arguing. I can make out two distinct voices, a man and a woman, in the middle of a fierce quarrel. Cats squabble. Fleas might tease and clamber over each other in a vain attempt to stay in the right. The light. A conceited and attentive kind of God one must try to appease to try and be eternally in the right. Most likely jittering about with 'God is within you' on their lips when what they really mean is 'God is within me'. Clinging to idealism to lose every duel to pragmatism. Deluded and without introspection finds himself being nailed through every part of his anatomy onto a cross of self-relative ideals. Constantly bringing about their position by asking the position of another, just so they have a reason to be defensive about an ideology that is as thin as the rain that falls on their cesspit of conceited and futile narcissism.

We follow the voices. Naturally, we follow the voices, because the other way is silence, the unknown. If faced towards the flaming gates of hell, Hercules with all his might, holding the sword of Damocles, the fingers of Athena could be wrapped roughly around my neck, he could be screaming the requiem of Anne Frank as she lay dying of typhus, the dust, the debris of her frightened sister. I for one would face down nightmare incarnate than face the darkness, again. Because for those of us that had the obnoxious bravado to try and walk away from red and into black do not choose it a second time. Nothing is so frightening to me as nothing. To not exist. Pre-birth. I could kill myself and this could all come to an abrupt and definitive end but it is nothing compared to existing in darkness. Pure black.

Darkness is not an option.

We follow the arguing couple; we can't catch up...

No matter how fast we walk, they seem to walk faster. Always getting further away, so after a while, we give up trying to track them down...

So, we walk away.

But I can still hear the bickering as if it echoes inside my head. All the finer points of modern culture have manifested themselves physically, a pointed, serrated weapon. But only the individual can use it and only on oneself. Stab, stab with force of muscle and monster on delicate pale flesh, on veiny arms. The voices grow louder still; they will not go away.

The structure and authority of my mind seems to being taken over. The voices are getting louder.

"Why are we arguing?" Involuntary reflex.

I can hear the voices getting louder. But it isn't coming from inside. The couple, the bickering couple that we were trying to follow are now following us. Walking faster than us. With more purpose. I am overcome by dread and fear. I panic and we increase our pace, walking ever faster.

Advancing, the man walking with longer strides closes his gap on us.

Terror has seized me. Wild eyed and furious I lunge at my assailer and the mad beads of cold sweat lend weight to the magnitude of my failure as my lightning forked actions spark no fire and I am brushed aside.

The monster touches the head of my love.

And the dream is over.

Sleep.

But it is not.

And I am struggling to separate my dreams from reality.

Elizabeth and Rachael Strawnford Meet for Dinner

It was far from the style of Rachael to want to meet anywhere but in public where she could be seen and admired by all. She chose a table near the centre of the room, erect, half with her gaze on me and the other half of her attention directed to the rest of the world, to which she would have doubt, was centred on her.

"There is a great deal to be said of dining in the head," Mulled Rachael, casting a languid gaze upon me without any real intend to invoke emotion, her thick eyes lashes seemed to reach out to me and pull me.

"You can speak for yourself Rachael, I don't particularly like to be found in public, in fact if it wasn't for the lure of such attractive company then I shouldn't be forced to bear such insipid coarse company vexing my brazen eyes," I can't help but stare back at the unwelcome company of the room.

"Attractive, well isn't that he most curious phrase you uttered of me since meeting?"

"Don't you think, most of the creatures in this room seem to be held to attention, I can hear Mars' drummers as I sit across from Athene."

"For all of your discontent demeanour you are determined to compliment me and I find it most flattering."

Hurriedly, the waitress served us our drinks. A scatty looking young think with curly dies blonde hair, she could not have been more than eighteen years old. I was indeed ready to order and wanted to have this entire ordeal over with as quickly as possible by Rachael waved her away. I took a sip of my orange juice and Rachael mulled amorously over her glass of prosecco.

"I hope you don't think it impudent of me to say but I did not think that you would one to drink prosecco"

"What would you picture me drinking?"

"Perhaps red wine"

"I drink to the room, if ever I were to find myself in such company that red wine the appropriate thing to drink then that is what I would drink, as it is, we are in a hovel being admired by ogres that believe that the height of society is a woman drinking cheap Italian wine because they have never been to Italy, they don't realise that the Italians wouldn't be caught dead drinking it and it is only the severely lacking in faculty that would pay for such a… classless decadent."

"You will have to forgive me, I don't follow, you don't seem to be 'severely lacking' in anything,"

"Because it makes me seem much more attainable to the gentlemen around us." She said this in such a flat tone that she seemed almost bored. "I expected you to drink orange juice though"

"I have never really understood drinking, I have spent a large part of my life dedicated to sharping my faculties, I don't understand why I should want to decrease them intermittently," This was the first self-assured thing I had said all evening.

"You must judge me a terrible wretch for indulging myself so," It seemed as if Rachael was feigning a wound while at the same time looking curiously and powerfully up from her drink.

I was a little startled by this challenge and replied with all of the genial modesty that I had, "not at all, I hold your entire demur in the highest of regards."

Rachael's expression only seemed to intensify as she began to stop being so intrigued by the rest of the room and I became increasingly interesting, "You are not much of an idealist. For all of your polished exterior and focus on progress it seems that you have no idea what you are progressing towards, nothing to strive for, a sheep lost in the wilderness. Perhaps you need taking in. Caesar salad, my darling and another glass," she said to the waitress who had appeared as Banquo might and made the turn of phrase look every bit as mysterious and damning as the first.

I ordered the same.

I paused for a long time, it seems like being a good person was nothing but a detriment to myself, I didn't have any other mantra for life, "I should like to be a good person," I realised then as I do now what a childlike response that was.

I thought that Rachael would have looked at me like a child in that moment, however it seemed to be the first time during the evening that she regarded me with any thought, perhaps she was regarding me as someone that she used to know in herself long ago, perhaps she sympathised with that position. She took a long, purposeful breath and took up.

"Do you believe in the nature of the soul Elizabeth?"

"I have read about it, but in all honesty, I have never found any solid reason for believing in it"

"Have people ever been particularly good to you, my love?"

I answered with a grave silence.

"Then if you don't do it for yourself and you don't do it for the people around you, then what reason could there be for being kind to the world? The simple answer is that you are doing it out of weakness. You perceive yourself as weak and as so you smile at the world in the conceited hope that it will smile back, but I think that you are beginning to understand that it won't. You're a clever girl, you can't fool yourself for long. However, you are stronger than you know. Physical domination is a thing of the past my darling, the new age is here and it is dominated by highly intelligent sociopaths and of you can't think as one who is dead inside then you shall become one who is dead in-side. It will cease to become an act and you shall walk in animation. As someone who intelligent though you can have safety."

"And what of moral progression? Am I to sit and stagnate, I have heard it said that the best thing that a girl can be in this world is pretty and dumb, I am not either of those things, so am I doomed?" now my gaze growing with hers.

The waitress smiled nervously as she lay our dinner on the table and asked us if we would require anything else. Rachael ordered me a prosecco, I objected, once and then she left to fetch me my drink.

"Let us suppose for just one second that heaven and hell does exist, god and the Lucifer are very real entities that will be plaguing an eternity after our death." Rachael began.

"I guess you want me to humour you and I will, okay, carry on."

"Do you consider yourself a good person? If your life were to end now, in our hypothetic example, would you enter heaven?"

"I have never hurt anyone in my life, though I shouldn't like to tell a being of omniscience how to judge me, if I were it, I would let me in"

"What an immaculately worded answer, if a soul were judged on linguistics you should live for an eternity in bliss. However, you are wrong, you're doomed to hell, as am I, from birth"

"I don't follow,"

"Heaven is a place for the righteous, but here we eat a chickens that lived their entire life in a cage, in all likelihood it never saw sunlight, it is a form of life that spends it's entire life screaming agony and depression, just so that we could save a little money on our dinner"

"That isn't really my fault though, what could I do?"

"You could not eat it, the entire system is called consumerism and enough people abstain for something then it changes, the system is run by sociopathic machines, they won't change for moral judgement but they will change if enough people exercise moral judgement. The fault and the onus lie with the individual."

The waitress delivered my drink that I accepted with a heavy heart. I pushed around my dinner and she continued.

"I don't suppose my princess has noticed but there is a lot of poverty in the world but we are sitting here drinking prosecco and eating like royalty"

"I didn't want prosecco-"

"Hush, hush darling. There is more than enough wealth in the world to go around but because so many of us live so large, we leave very little for the rest, our economy is allowed to live because we wring the air from the lungs of others. Our companies go-over sea and force people to work for almost nothing so that we can have designer clothes. Nike-slaves make our shoes and we complain about the colour of the laces, there is a lot of guilt to be placed on our shoulders."

"Is all of this solely aimed at making me feel guilty?"

"Quite the opposite, I want to tell you that it is time to disown a positive progression and own a negative progression. We are going to hell my dear and when I meet Lucifer, I would like him to think fondly of me. Treat people badly, the universe will think better of you for it, stop trying to be the best person that you can, the most agreeable and well thought of person. You indulge in ethics protect a metaphysical absurdity. Indulge debauchery and be free. We are all just passengers on this train to the grave, you make think it is better to travel in first class by yourself, but I assure you that it is far more fun in the second row."

I took a sip of my drink and felt a sickly sting in my throat, it tasted sour in my mouth but the second and third seemed to trickle down a little more gaily. I didn't enjoy it half as much as Rachael did though. She smiled at the young blonde attendant making poignant eye contact.

"I am meeting some friends in the zinc club this evening, over by the river, we are going to go and establish our-selves the social proprietors and dandies of our time. I don't think it should be your scene, not in what you are wearing at any rate. Wear something grabbing next time and I shall introduce you to them. Message me, I have enjoyed speaking with you," Rachael seemed solemn to the point of disappointment in rounding our evening off.

"I shall think about it," was my response, however in truth there was nothing to think about.

Our evening wound down as we finished our drinks and extended to each other civilities and the romances of the twenty first century.

I began to wonder what a rose would look like without a thorn. Is it possible to find beauty without contradiction? Perhaps beauty is triumphing against overwhelming odds. There is nothing quite so cathartic as being cut by something alluring. I want to dance in fields of thorns turn perpetually until a great puppeteer pulls them above head, turning each movement into a lifetime of toil stretching among stars. Galaxies hall live and die in an instant and I will my life to the whims of the breeze. I will understand the meaning behind shadow and be at one with existence. The rules of physics shall no longer be a half caste matrix as I understand the true essence love, hate and beauty. I shall embrace honesty and feel justice while fire overcomes my body and shall see courage and feeling in the smallest of existence as the mighty brazen monsters seem not to stir an inch in the millennia, they torture a reflection of an echo.

Shadows

"Hello Gael… It has been quite some time. I have come to speak with you again." My voice is grave and catches on the shrouded, unseen words that I can taste in the air. I must compose myself. I can only imagine the magnitude of grief that seeing me again is going to cause him. So, I stand in the light that protrudes through the door. A great wretched outline of darkness leaning against the door frame: Chronos has come. The ticking hand of time has come full circle, looks for the next minute-mark in the eyes of a lost little boy hiding in his dark room.

I stand against the backdrop for some time, finding myself calling out with little conscious effort, "Gael!" With a loud voice: rasping, before calling gently, "Where are you?" But my voice is overtaken by the tyrannous darkness, holding the state tight with both hands.

"Where am I lizzie?" Gail's voice is stoic and trails off… I stand as still as the air until his voice appears again from the gloom, "Where are you… Where were you lizzie?" Gael snaps in jovial, manic, elation before catching himself, as one stares over a cliff into an abys.

"It doesn't matter where I have been Gael, I am here now," I try to make my voice friendly; calm relaxed, soothing, harmonious… But the words turn to discords; the hard, cold air breathes and the words rot, turn stale and are cut dead from the air.

"Where were you lizzie?"

"I- I couldn't come to see you. I was told- We thought that you might do better if you had some time by yourself. Without me…" And for the first time in my life, I lied to Gael, "To help you."

"Help me? You abandoned me! I have been so lonely…" Gael's voice fades out into low sobs. His short breathes stab at the distance between us and inevitably misses the mark as he hits me, the strike had to travel a long time in order to reach. We have grown apart; perhaps I stayed away for too long.

"I am sorry I wasn't there for you, Gael," I speak soft and as distant as Gael as my little brother has become to me.

"You weren't there for me Lizzie because you were too busy being a whore!" Gale's voice becomes angry, agitated but almost monotone, "You fucking whore! You don't know the meaning of the word responsibility! But I do. Responsibility is looking after someone and you didn't look after me Lizzie! You let Savage nearly kill me," then Gael's voice changes tone, he becomes almost unsure of himself, "In some ways he did kill me…"

"Look- Gael," and the raging injustice that I have wrought upon this child hits me, "I was trying to be a human being in a world full of monsters. I didn't- I didn't- You know- Where the fuck were you Gael? Huh? Put me to your impossible standards? Where the fuck were you? You were meant to protect me, keep me clean. Cogent little shit. Who are you to judge me? Where were you? It was you that wanted to push on, I wanted to go back, be," and I mimic his voice, "'Responsible', but you ran."

I slump from my powerful figure of adult authority, standing proud in the door frame, to a smaller- more delicate and frail fae that huddles in her own failure. Huddles into something a little truer. My smaller frame looks so much smaller as a large amount of light burst through the empty space that I no longer occupy. The light shines straight onto Gael who is sitting on the floor with his back to the wall, his knees protruding from the ground in an image of defeat. His face is buried in his forearms which are wrapped around his legs as if he were being carried away by a sea of troubles, he is trying to hold on to the one tree that could carry him away from his storm. I see him there and I don't feel so alone in my anguish. His pain reflects mine…

"How could I protect you, Lizzie? I am just a kid, right? I tried to protect you, remember? But the man was too strong, he hurt me and made me bleed," Gael's face, as he reaches for his scar, is wide eyed and full of pain. He is remembering, the light shining on his face lights up those memories and even if I had not lived them with him, I could read them in his eyes. An angel was hiding in my shadow, "What were you doing before I came in?"

"Has nobody told you?" And I contemplate telling Gael that I was almost raped…

"Told me what? Mum said that you are a whore and a bad person and that I shouldn't go near you."

There is a daemon in the room, malevolent and clever. It is passing between us, he has secrets and where he treads, only flaming ruins are left.

"That isn't right Gael. You are right, we should have gone home. But I didn't for a moment think that we were in any danger. I wanted an adventure, I didn't know-"

Gael stops me in my clueless summaries with a low whisper, "you don't know," and it is all I can do to just listen, "You don't know what it has been like since what happened- happened. It hurts. The scar. It still hurts. They said it would stop hurting and they give me the pain killers and I take them. All the time. But I think about it, all the time. And it still hurts. All the time. And he is there when I close my eyes, Lizzie! And the blood. My blood! I can see it, I still feel it, pouring down my chest. No amount of water washes it off. No medicine is taking it away. My dreams scream. My mind aches. I am tired. I am sick and tired of always feeling sick and tired, Lizzie." Gael's voice trails off a languid walk of misery. He begins to cry and each tear is further tarnishing his already dirty yellow brick road. Those bricks, once golden as a griffin's beak- prosperous. I used to look after that shining beacon of light, it used to light up my own life, use it as a guide. I should never have imagined that I would be the one to extinguish that light.

The Bathtub Laughs

Ceramic. Cool, white, pristine. The walls are perfect teeth, encroaching- chattering a shivering micrographia. Speaking and shrieking a sulphur madness; I shake with nervous anticipation. I am a leaf on a tree, holding on desperately to the branch. My branch. My small, trembling hands with their delicate and petite fingers are holding on… My tree is about to lose its last leaf.

Do the walls hear me?

See me…

If these walls could talk, they would tell me I am weak, say that my frail frame is a result of my inability to look after myself. The result of the heavy ceiling, crushing me.

"Cowering, conceited, empty shell. The potential you threw away! Self-centred. Hollow failure, bring the agony upon yourself. Admit it! Your pain is your own doing and no one is going to help you because you don't deserve it. You don't feel enough pain. Should have died a long time ago; nothing but a burden. A blemish. Crying failure."

"Ha ha ha," The bathtub laughs. Like it had been smiling for a while but that little chuckle is all that slipped out. But I can't fault how it looks. Sleek and smooth, it is clear that it has been looking after its skin, which is more than I can say for myself. So, I don't feel that I have the right to step but, lest it pulls rank. Rises above me. Everything I touch falls down. Then I try to stand up, I fall. I try to stand in something clean and I fall, this place is too pure. It knows that I am not clean, that I don't belong and it is casting me out, not allowing me to stand up. But it is a game, each time I try to stand and fall, laughter.

The floor is cold. White tiles. One after another: A perfect little pattern of perfect square divinity. A beautiful effigy to the simple little child-like nature than once grew within me. The naïve child is shoved up against a wall and forced to play games with flesh licking ladies. My skin, no longer perfect and soft but brittle and cracked. The words hang in my head and shatter like waves breaking on rocks. Like a crackling fire, burning alone. The forest of frost has one less icicle, I have fallen. I am broken on the frenzied path of fungi. Resigned to sit there, the path leads to nowhere.

My knees hurt. My knees are cold. Bare, I cradle here. My knees hurt.

This frail form is being mocked: wall to wall.

They are whispering about me…

"Too slight," mumbles the toilet.

"No breasts," replies the hand rail in agreement. Those two are toxic together.

"No man that has ever walked in here would want this plain sheet, nor anywhere else I have overseen," The light fixture looks down on me, talks like it knows it is better than me.

"No curves."

"Body of a child."

I have the countenance and the balloon-like frail soul of a child. My heart is empty and shut.

"You are incapable of making new relationships."

It is true, I am a closed shell, an empty heart and I feel like I am without a home.

Made for rape. No love. No comfort. No sleep. No smile. No-

The small tile straining against my pressured knee cracks. What was once white is now black. Forever scarred.

I rise to my feet and my fear is turned placid; a feeling of assured decision quenches me. No chattering between tiny white monsters but a peace, a miracle blanket is comforting my existential reaching soul.

Opening the doors of the medicine cabinet, the doors are brown. Perhaps it is an effect of the bathroom, one of its tricks, just a veil of emotions that I have had pulled over me, but the doors look faintly red. The colours of doors is an awfully dull subject right now. I have been writing myself. Perhaps If I could just remember the words…

A blanket of pain snuggled under my breast,

Fear is near when comparing the other side,

But to its self: fear is the blanket of black,

Spend too long and darkness is what you become,

Being darkness, I am destroyed by the light,

No one can see me in the darkness though,

Invisible; people will look right through me,

Through the empty, faded, soulless black abyss,

If I die now, shall I return to the dark?

Would I die or would I reincarnate back,

To forever wallow and be familiar…

I am not finished yet.

Red is not a colour that likes to rest. Ceaselessly borne back to mind: a siren, a warning. Red is growing fear. Hungry fires, unquenchable. Tonight, this city will burn.

Furrowing frantically, my father's disposable razor eventually steps forward. It is plastic. A monument to the manufactured misery that engulfs my chastised mind. I can feel my heart beat. Laboured double beats scraping on the vertebrae of time. Flowing like water across my wide eyes: The Styx.

My hand does not shake as I put the plastic tip in between a towel. I wonder how many people have done this before. Countless. The plastic breaks. When I was a little girl, I would get lego stuck together too tight and I couldn't open it again. I would give it to my mother and she would undo them for me with a knife. My razor blade sounds like lego. Rummaging through the towel, I find my treasure.

The small blade feels cold in my hand, placed delicately between my thumb and index finger. I am become Tamora, with sickly schemes for flayed skin, blood and vengeance. Vengeance against myself- for being me. To wreak havoc on the plain and barren canvas for being so plain and barren. This colourless canvas knows no joy, no love and elicits no colour that would be painted by an artist's loving hand. Uninspired.

I push my back against the wall and hold out my wrist. Like an offering. Like it will bring my family back. Some God somewhere must have been disappointed with my offering because I received no relief. Perhaps the God I prayed to was too sickly to do anything but watch. Perhaps the God that I am praying to enjoys this spectacle, grief is its life blood and is pleased, it would reward me with more grief. A singular black line running through the universe.

The pain is incidental. The small and sharp searing pain is a welcome relief. Physical pain, something else to contrast the incessant screaming darkness banging on the walls of my head. It flows around my body, making my blood darker, always in pain but no marks. No help. No sympathetic voice to-

HOW DO YOU NOT KNOW!?

The physical pain is no more than a manifestation of mental anguish. Not worth noting. Its only reason for existence is mounded on the dark side of some snowy mountain, desolate and secluded.

It is the first time that I have cut myself and I don't know what to do. "Did I do it right?" "Is it deep enough?" So, I saw deeper. The crimson nightmare now drenches my pale skin and drips spots of huddled misery onto the white tiles and one such splash buries its self in the cracked tile.

I am the inconsequential offering to Pallas.

The drum beat in my head, my mouth and in my chest continues its heralding drone. I am thinking

the mad, incoherent, panicked thoughts of a court jester, being hung from the neck.

The bath tub thinks that my antics are funny. It continues to laugh at me, making my one-woman performance a shining beacon of whimsy. The beacon rises out of my gawping mouth as my head is raised to heaven, until it reaches the ceiling, where it bursts into fire. The fire catches and before I know it, the drapes are laughing at me too. The wall tiles, the bath tub and the drapes, anything with the slightest hint of narcissistic loathing is raising a chorus. The basin is trying to laugh too, but it can't. The basin is choking on my blood, but it looks positively elated. Enraptured with antipathy, enamoured with wells full to the brim with tailor made hate and ecstasy.

The bleeding has almost stopped or at least it isn't pouring. I stagger into the hallway where darkness is the constant. The air is still. Shadows dance across the wall as I fumble back to my room. I open the door, close it again and cling to the back of it. Shame washes over me. Head to toe, bathed in the knowledge that my body shall never look the same again.

Finding a scrunchie, I wrap it twice around my wrist. I fall asleep. Effortlessly.

The next morning, I wake to find my wrist covered in dry blood. The scrunchie is soaked, my covers are marred. I spend some time, out of time, staring at it- stoic. Fading away from reality, my glossed eyes natural colour seems to fade. I look at the blood-stained bed I have made.

The Second Party (The Rabbit Hole)

"The roses in Patricia's hair are a withered and writhing, desperate plea for attention from a woman who clearly spends too much time sitting at a computer screen in a half dozen melancholy ecstasy. If this half animal- half sub human abomination was to spend some quality time in the real world, taking care and nurturing herself and her life then she might gain some experience. Some knowledge of flowers. Their smells, their features and flaws, their preferences. She might come to the realisation that the roses, have become tired- worn out, but bright pink- it makes her look like a hippo in a tutu."

"Fuck," said Rachael, shocked into consciousness with my outburst. I could see all the cogs and gears begin to yawn into motion as she looked vaguely and disinterestedly at Pat.

"It really is nothing short of blasphemy; life is full of majesty. Not just her brazen frivolity of flowers but of the grass! The sun, the books! The pain and sacrifice that artists have devoted entire lives to, to be ignored. To be given life and then sit ignorant of its passing. If God exists, then he moves through poetry. This woman can barely read, how could she have any notion of the nature of God?"

"Perhaps she doesn't believe in God," retorted Rachael.

"I doubt that she believes in much that isn't put on a plate in front of her face. Besides, nihilism isn't the answer, it is a substitute- like a sick note. 'Please insert something to believe in here'. And Patricia isn't a nihilist, she is just ignorant"

Rachael looks unphased, her demeanour is quiet and relaxed, as is the status quo. I search her face extensively, trying to find some evidence of approval, some small sign that she relates to me. But no such encouragement is coming. Rachael takes her crumpled carton of cigarettes out from her jean pocket before taking heed of me. Like a crocodile, seeing some small animal struggling in its waters, she freezes mid-way through her languid swim. With the smallest of movement, she motions the box unto me with a tilt and a knowing, yet curious half glare, half smile.

"Thank you," I take a cigarette from the carton.

"I didn't take you for a smoker," But she knows.

"I guess I am not the only one in the habit of assuming things then," She seems to almost wince at my angled blow, but Rachael is a glacier.

She holds the light to my wide eyes face and I light up red as a whore on a cold night. I am pretty sure that I just put my lips around the end and suck it. The spark catches and take my first drag. I can feel its smoky discharge trying to force its way down my throat. But it gets stuck in my oesophagus, it is too much to take in all at once and I have a physical reaction, a convulsion. I bring it back up and spit it out with a splutter and a poignant dejected look stuck to my face as look up at Rachael. Rachael doesn't laugh and doesn't reprimand me. She just smirks and looks satisfied.

"You don't have to Lizzie, I'm not-"

"Shut up!" I exclaim, gasping for air.

I wrap my lips around Rachael's cigarette once more and briefly observe the words 'superking' printed on the side. This time I manage to keep it down, all the way into my lungs. But I have the same problem once more and my body convulses, and I am forced to spit it up in a dissonance of messy, inelegant actions. This time Rachael looks at me with concern but doesn't say anything as I continue to drag until I stop coughing…

"I am guessing that you wouldn't want to talk to Pat or Michael then?" Rachael solemnly throws away like litter.

"I assure you, that despite what you may think of me, that I am perfectly capable of being amiable"

"Perhaps excitable would be a more accurate word for current mood," Retorts Rachael.

"Well," as my eyes widen and I make some wild grandiose gesture with my hand, "let us see, shall we not?" I turn to catch Pat's eye from across the garden, Pat is thirsty for attention and I catch her eye almost immediately, "Pat, oh Pat-darling- we need you, meander on over here my darling."

Rachael shoots me an uneasy glance but I swerve it and greet Pat with wide eyes, a wild smile, teeth baring easily and seductively in my den.

"It is good to see you Pat, don't look so discerned, you positively look like a fish out of water and that won't do, please, let us go and sit down, you must be exhausted," I keep my unblinking eyes on Pat, I can only imagine that this is the kind of exhilaration that a psychopath must feel, stumbling upon a wounded animal after following its trail of blood. Rachael says nothing but smiles uneasily at Pat. Pat fails to detect any feeling of discomfort from Rachael and instead, the little that Rachael gave, acted as permission to relax. Pat exhales and relaxes as I sit opposite her, my chin in my hands my entire body gravitating towards her. Rachael reluctantly sits down and between us we exchange all the usual pleasantries: hugs and kisses. It was electrifying. I once even smiled and playfully struck pat on the arm as she flapped her jaw open so often and so wide that I could see all of the colour inside of her mouth and all of her malformed teeth.

"I just couldn't believe that Jason," another innocuous character from another innocuous soap opera, "would try and get back in to his babies' life!" Pat yawned, showing off her impressive jaw.

"Oh, but a father must make an effort to be in their child's life," Rachael played.

"But he doesn't even have a job!" Blurted Pat.

Rachael let this burst of uncontrolled ignorance stay silent in the air, but I felt that I needed to know a little more about where this thread came from.

"Oh, no? is a person's profession or lack of profession of particular consequence to the individual?" Rachael sees me giving pat a little rope and she looks uneasy but covers it up in her traditional laissez faire over coat. Now I feel like a hunter of big game. I have my pith helmet on, rifle, cleverly concealed at my back and even a rather large knife hidden up my sleeve. I sit back in my chair and aim my rifle. Stiff and as cold as stone and her yawing just seems to become more brazen and more erratic.

"Well, if you don't have a job, then you are just not trying. Not con-tri-bu-" as she struggles to repeat her jungle mantra, "-ting to so-ciet-ee. If no body worked, then nothing would work, would it?" Perhaps Pat realised the kind of den that she was in at that point, but I think it more likely that she just forgot her lines.

"That is a very interesting theory that you have there Pat, did you come up with that all by yourself? I bet a little bird told you!" I rest my head back on my hand, but my eyes are fully open. Leaning in, as I am, enjoying every word with reverent adulation. Rachael seems a little distressed though with the entire role-playing exercise. I had never picked Rachael as the charitable kind, but here she is, protecting big game. Game that is in abundance, it should be noted. If a suitable replacement could be found for my game of double entendre, it most certainly would be to destroy this thing. Removing one could decrease the surplus population and after all, then will just end up eating themselves and each other if left without predators in the area.

"Oh, Patricia, you have the quaintest, most adorable ideas on the running of a country, truly political mind. What do you do day-to-day?"

Pat explained that she worked as a waitress in a small café and had done for the entire of her working life after leaving school at 16 without qualifications and without an education.

"What a small watering hole that you do frequent," I said, leaning in, further still, "perhaps one day you shall be eaten by a lion! But until then, I fancy your everyday fight for survival to be all the toil possible for such rough… hands." I smile with self-endearing adulation, but now I feel the game has run its course and I should get bored to pursue it any further. I feel like I am hunting an animal, however I have found this one floundering helplessly on its back. Kicking her legs helplessly in the air, barking half-baked ideological drivel; leaned from the tortoise next to her, who is also laying on her back- floundering, spewing the drivel learned from the older animal next to her, learned from the row of tiny graves. The headstones have no names as their words forked no lightning. It is difficult to tell if the message came from the line of tiny graves, or from the aging pack of wolves, who in turn have their own line of slightly larger, nameless graves.

We then pretend to be friends. Kiss and cuddle. The show, before we move on to the next scene. We saunter at an awkward pace, distorted shapes of the human race scrawl themselves into existence, dis coloured and glittering a reluctant bourgeois connection to reality. I think about love. How to fall in love. The barriers around my heart and the little death the erupts with every breath. The same at the start as at the end.

Rachael tells me, "I feel like I am dying when I am falling in love and I feel like I am dying when I fall out of love. Dying, in all sense of the word- not just a physical death but a death inside. I can feel spontaneous adulation dying. It is the small encounters that stick out in my mind. Joy of meeting a friend, flutter of my heart, energy rising through my chest that rises so high that it shapes my mouth to smile. It goes away! I must fake it. Fake not being broken. Fake the joy that people come to experience. Or they go away. Then you are dying lonely, because no one will talk to you. No angels to rescue those dying inside. Just prejudice. People resent you, like a leper" She laughs nervously to herself, "Don't be afraid Lizzie, if you can feel your soul slipping through your fingers, then that means you still have a soul. Don't play games, live in the now-"

"I am living in the now," I begin, "moving the hands of the clock, turning the gears, making the world around me move"

Rachael looks displeased, she turns away from me. She looks despairingly inside, searching... "It sounds like you are playing at God. How could you possibly be living if you are orchestrating? You can play video games on your phone. But here, you can live. You meet people, you listen to them and they change your perspective," She implores, "the way you think: Everyone is an NPC and it is just you that is playing! The world doesn't work like that. Everyone is alive, living with their own personal bubble, just like yours. So, you are connected, you have the same bubbles, but if you don't learn to see your universe as our universe then your perspective is going to be very small. You wouldn't be unique either, there are droves of people out there that think that they create reality, that it wouldn't happen without them." Assuredly, she looks into my eyes, "Those people live lonely lives. Everyone knows that they are not intelligent because they can't even see out of their own box. I don't believe that Patricia is any different to such a person. I just think Patricia has a place in our spider web, I know lots of good people that Patricia has introduced me to."

I tell Rachael that it sounds like she is using Patricia to her own selfish ends, just like me, "At least my ends are interesting; original. You use people like a garden variety robot".

"You flatter yourself with an idealistic and misguided view on reality. You flatter yourself to think you can orchestrate anything remotely interesting. If you continue to burn these bridges then you will live on an island by yourself. Then you can live there on your lonesome, be the most intelligent person there! And play with yourself all day."

"Hey, Fuck you Rachael," I keep a calm front, but my heart gives me away. I am agitation incarnate.

"And I am not using Patricia," Rachael continues, "I don't have any plans or designs. I am trying to live in the moment, be a part of the spider web, part of something bigger than me. So, fuck you right back Elizabeth. See you around."

That was an interesting conversation. Rachael disappears into a cloud of obnoxious social justice. Self-assured lioness.

………………………………………………………………
………………………………………………………………
………………………………..

The lights are blinding my eyes.

I can feel the dejected butterflies fluttering around my stomach. They are flying up to my breast. Butterflies of green… their delicate wings flap and float away. Up and out of my mouth into the open air. The jealousy exhaled; poison released into the air where it could breed. Once it has bred, I would need to inhale again, and what I would breathe would be a more violent and vicious. Poison. Deformed melancholy, a flawed colour, frustrated by what I understand of spectrum. Slowly it melts, just like the other colours, and runs. Drips down into my stomach. Food for hungry insects to feast on. The caterpillars get fat, form cocoons of vile black, expand. Gives birth to the sick, deformed, shimmering emerald butterflies. They have flown once already tonight, into full view where they withered. There still feels like there is substance, life festering within the pit. Squirming and wriggling in my bowels. It is making me very sick.

My enthusiastic countenance: a self-centred yet amiable self-assurance has dissolved into a hysteria of boiling, burning neutralisation. Fuck this abomination; childish bravado. I can't be here anymore. There are wasps in my head. Buzz buzz you juvenile coward. That's the way it is. Try and fly around the head, that's where the knowledge is. Fly and keep air borne. If you stop, you will die.

The lights are blinding my eyes.

I am pushing past people, shoulder to shoulder. We are all packed in this party like sardines in a tin can.

People pushing by, and now I am a breeze, scurrying off into the night.

The night isn't dark. It is a sky full of stars. Whites of eyes looking out from damp and inviting coves. Wide eyes angels and devils dancing.

Lightning inspired, thunder roaring chorus, rises in tremendous crescendos of bass. Opening and closing as curtains close for roaring darkness and open again in perfect rhythm to the rise and fall so that it lets in the lights that are blinding my eyes!

I sway from side to side. I feel electric as the music moves through me. I feel alive.

I listen to music and it reminds me that the world isn't just a concrete jungle. That there is something more, something inside, something vulnerable, weak, something that swells and feels and knows that all the greed and all the mechanical-marching towards death, it isn't real. The structure, the walls that cage me, the manacles that bound me- They come from the outside and the truth comes from the inside, no one could ever take the thoughts from inside my head. I can't be defeated by anyone but myself. Do you ever feel like that? I am more that…

A faint voice from far away calls, "Can I buy you a drink?" When I open my eyes, I see the least modest picture of juvenile youth, most modest of stature, straining to appease a base desire to procreate. He smiles a dead and hopeful smile. I am entirely repulsed. I tell him, "No," in no uncertain terms but he won't leave my company. The smiling, colourful insect, with his cross patterned red shirt, he is a shark. I must be bleeding.

I try to ignore him.

I close my eyes and try to become part of the music again. The energy begins to run through me before being sapped out from the contact of someone pressing up behind me... I stop in my world to briefly enter his. I turn and look to him, beckon him to come a little closer... he does and as I lean into him and his eyes are wide, and his heart is pounding. I punch him in his foolish and now crooked nose.

He reels back, startled and shocked. Then crimson glory begins to fall. He looks like a four-year-old with a nose bleed. A statue to mourn the ignorant. Then he flees into the night. Into the darkness, and I am alone again. I didn't feel alone until unwanted company. I would sooner be alone and in pain than be the victim of social obligation. These chains around my wrists, tugging me here and there, dig in tight. I have just lost the ambition to feed or feel my soul. It feels like there is a void. So, I stop moving. I look at the crowd of wide-eyed zombies and leave their ranks.

Hands in my pockets- I walk deflated but laissez faire; kick my feet about the air. Like a ghost, bored with ethereal existence, my mind turns to matters of interest and I wonder where Rachael could be. This is all beginning to look like an exercise in futility. I hate being alone. I hate feeling like there is no one to relate to. Like I am a human in a world of robots;

like a monster among fluffy clouds. All I am good for is abuse. Feeling like all relationships: abuse and take, alternatively, until one of us has had enough.

"You hit that boy very hard, I don't think he shall be coming back here anytime soon. In fact, I am afraid to be in your vicinity."

"-Mr Darcy, what deity have I offended to deserve your company?"

"Any God that propriates peace, I think," Michael smiles, evidently pleased with his quip. I reluctantly smile and feel a little disarmed. I brush the hair away from my face, an involuntary motion and if I could curdle from it, then I would fold myself indefinitely to have more control over myself. Michael does not disgust me half as much as the young man in question though. I fear I shall be amiable in his company.

"I am not having a good time," I start, "I feel disgusted with the company. I feel alienated. Why do people come here?"

"To get drunk," Michael replies.

"And does that help? -With the darkness"

"Everything is dark here… If you didn't want darkness, you should not have come here"

"That is not what I meant, what I meant was: Does it make you feel worse?"

Michael pauses, as if he has not thought on this before, or perhaps recovering something long since conceived. "Yes, it makes you feel worse. But that is the point. I guess we have given up on 'feeling better'," Michael makes 'air commas' with his fingers, to which I feel physically repulsed, "we come here to be around awful people, hide in the dark and sulphurous wastes, because that is what we are. We are children of Bacchus! It makes no sense for us to try and better ourselves, there is no redemption. We linger in the darkness because darkness is what we are. You look as if you have a little bit of the darkness about you too…" Michael trails off.

"I think you might be right. I haven't felt quite like myself lately. I am not sure I fit in here though. There does not seem to be many people here I would like to talk to. I have run out of words to say at any rate."

"Perhaps you just aren't giving it a fair chance, would you like a drink?" Michael raises his bushy eye brows and makes an open-handed gesture. It is as inviting as it is juvenile.

"Narcissus," I mutter under my breath. To be so self-obsessed and so unsatisfied. Self-loving yet self-loathing. The entire facade takes place in a small box in the corner of the mind. The allure of that perspective, the degree to which people drink, few ever step back from that mirror. Most just perpetuate around it, finding new ways to look at themselves. At myself too. Until eventually, I find myself asking if there ever was, ever could be another way of looking at things. Are there eyes to look through but these? The truth is, that there is more than the mirror. There is more than sight!

There is action and people can live as fulfilled in action as in sight. There are people do what calls to them. But that isn't me right now. I am still sitting in my box. I just moved around a little and now I can see the reflection of the people around me. It is surprising, how similar we look. I rarely look inside the glass if I am not in the frame. I expect those around me to stop moving when I am not near.

"I am sorry?" Michael says a little perplexed.

"Okay then, Michael, I shall sit in darkness with you."

"I am glad to hear it, what would you like?"

Of course, there is more than one type of drink. I would feel embarrassed to tell Michael that I don't drink. Besides, if I am going to play with monsters under the table, then I would prefer them not to know that I don't belong here.

"Gin and tonic please Michael," I order what my mother drinks.

"Hendrix or pink?"

I pretend to be disinterested and tell him, "Don't be silly," and apparently that was the right answer, "Do you mind if we sit down?" I ask.

"I wouldn't have it any other way," says Michael.

Patricia Tells a Story About Michael

"I couldn't believe just how much she had changed, but how how much she looked the same. I almost walked right past her; she didn't even look at me." Patricia was engaged in telling one her remote and suspect stories about an event that may or may not have taken place. It most certainly didn't happen the way she regales it, if it happened at all.

"Her hair was bright red and she had a nose ring in! I couldn't believe it, just sittin' there, out the front of the coffee shop. I only recognised her because she still has that far off look she gets when no one is talking to her."

I can't imagine anyone doing Patricia the disservice…

"So, I just *had* to stop and talk to her, "Hey Glory," I said. But she didn't even seem to recognise *me* at first, she just kind of stared through me, like she couldn't remember who I was, "Hello Patricia, it has been some time," 'Some time'? Yeah, like, years! She still speaks with that calm and eloquent 'I'm too clever to have fun' voice that she always had. I love that silly bitch, she was sitting with her perfect little figure, her hair so prim and sensible. I don't know how she always looks so small and fragile, because inside, she is not fragile, she is a scary woman! Even sitting down on her own, I was scared to approach her. We soon got to talking about baking, it really was the only thing that we ever had in common. She said that she had just finished making a friend an *'Apricot Icing Fruit Cake'* that apparently, I would *'just die for'*. It was quite a scary choice of words but I wasn't fazed at all. I told her that I have been changing the kind of jam that have been putting in my tarts and she seemed dead-impressed with that! Haha…" Patricia seems to trail off in a dusty haze of neuroticism and self-loathing, most probably trying to piece together all of the parts of her story into something that made sense and come to a point. I find it perilously difficult, to the point of dangerous, for my health and sanity to listen to the woman talk for too long. A slight change in the wind is likely to distract me from her conversation.

"She said that she had not seen Michael in a long time," I feel the icy cold fingers of fate on the back of my neck as whatever demon that had me occupied handed me over to another dark entrenchment.. I find myself awake and listening to Patricia's every imperative word, "I don't know why, I felt the need to say it. Sometimes when she looks at me, she doesn't say anything. And it makes me sad. It makes me nervous. I get scared and I don't know why I said it..." Patricia looked like she was on the verge of tears. She was getting very hot and upset. Beaming red like a bloated beetroot with two disappointed circles protruding from her face, she didn't seem like she wanted talk any more.

"It's alright Pat," Rachael puts a sympathetic arm around her friend, "You did nothing wrong." Rachael kisses Patricia on the cheek and Patricia's flustered composition transcends shame and she puts on a bashful smile. She looks a little lighter of heart and lighter of face now. Rachael, by stark contrast, looks as disconnected as ever.

Our small group of children masquerading as adults consists of the aforementioned party and two accomplices of Rachael's: Katrina; a small reserved girl, mousy hair, big brown eyes that shone brazen beyond their position, wonderfully introspective and reserve, however not particularly well read. The other is Ruby. Ruby is a burn-out. Half inebriated; half inconvenient truths. Ruby is the living embodiment of Icarus. Presently, Ruby is stealing swigs from a hip flask in an inauspicious attempt to conceal the act.

Our small company was quiet for a time after Patricia's story. I was burning. I had a question that I felt needed answering. But not here, not like this.

Not from Patricia's lips.

The evening beat on. Patricia and the half-inebriated girl drunk some more. They made themselves scarce from the rest of the group- as little girls tend to do: To make some casual remarks of derision about members of the group present or at very least putting the rest of the group on edge from such a threat, which of course is where the power in the separation lay. Or such is where my insecure mind tends to wander to- paranoia. Perhaps I am jealous of the familiarity. As it is, I wish that I had someone that I could take to my room to show a little piece of writing I have quipped or interesting little pieces of sentiment that I could show. The two girls are currently putting my contemptuous attitude to shame, trying on each other's clothes and drinking Prosecco. Regardless, it was obvious form the high-pitched giggling and loud footfalls that the two girls had no immediate intention of returning to the group. So, I used this opportunity to ask a question…

"Katrina, you are so wonderfully quiet, I hope that I haven't offended you in some way, I am told I have a tendency for doing so," The vowels… too much enunciation or too little, it comes out as derivative. So, I look her in the eye and smile a reassuring smile and she searches for anything in the room to look at that isn't into my eyes. I toss a casual sideways glance at my companion in the room, Rachael, for validity. However, Rachael isn't the kind of friend that blindly follows your poor life choices unless she has a reason for doing so. She does not give me validation in my games; however she knows what I am referring to and smiles to herself and no one else. Her individuality is the thing that I like best about her.

Katrina's eyes search the floor for words to say, "...I am sorry Elizabeth, I didn't mean to make you feel detestable in anyway. I am just the kind of person that would rather listen than to speak," Katrina's eyes glance up to meet my own unwavering gaze before scurrying away again.

Her answer surprises me in its agreeableness that juxtaposes the sarcasm of it, "Not at all," I sincerely proceed, "I just wanted to make sure that I had not offended you in some way, I like you, Katrina, I would like to be friends," this time when our eyes meet, I make sure I smile, and even though I know she is not looking at my eyes, she knows that I am smiling, my eyes beam with elation and she can feel the genuine warmth in me at this moment in time. She returns the sentiment a thousand-fold in the smallest twitches of her face; her shoulders do not seem so rigid now. For the first time in the evening, I feel like I am in a party of three.

"However, as amiable as this conversation is, I must ask it to diverge. I don't ask for much, just information or even the elaboration of a story. You see, the previous conversation, when our party was larger, was not as large as it seemed. I am afraid I was in the dark for the entirety of the conversion. I have not had the privilege of meeting 'Glory'; nor did Michael mention her… in all truth, this is the first time I have heard her mentioned," For a moment, Rachael looks like Katrina and they exchange uneasy looks. Meanwhile, I sit patiently as the silence sits patiently on the floor between all three of us. Even the bustle in the next room has died to a dull roar.

At length, Rachael begins, each word chosen precisely and pronounced as if making a mistake here could be costly, "Katrina, you knew Gloria far better than I did, why don't you regale us?" History between Rachael and Gloria must have been severe as I have never seen Rachael dodge an opportunity to assume responsibility. Rachael's eyes are fixed on Katrina, cold and as certain as death. It is clear that neither woman wished to talk about her. In turn, Katrina, though still timid as a shrew in the dead of night, holds Rachael's gaze from beneath her brow.

"I don't see why I should," Katrina's small voice carries with it the smallest rumblings of thunder, however does not stand taller than a child. The words fall from the air to be replaced by, "But I shall," Katrina admits in a reluctant whisper.

"I first met Glory when I was at school. She was the year below me. Half shy; half assertive. She was a social magnet. Never imposed herself on anyone or anything. Remarkably, it was as if people just gravitated toward her. I found it astonishing too," Katrina smiles, "I was very quiet in school. I preferred to stay in the library and read instead of diving into social politics. One day in the library, as I sat in my favourite chair, I noticed someone else in my usual desolation. I took no notice; it was like strangers to flit and flirt in and out of my comfort blanket. But the individual persisted to sit and read for months. One day, as I was finishing reading for the afternoon, the girl approached me. Though I had been aware of the presence of someone new, I had no inkling as to who it was. I was always far too nervous to make eye contact, so as she approached, the blood in my veins turned to ice and I froze. I knew who she was the moment she started talking to me. I believe the conversation unfolded a little like this…

"Hello there, I didn't mean to startle you," she looked at me without pity, maintained her independent disposition and smiled. At once, I felt a benevolence warm my icy countenance; I knew this was going to be my friend.

"Not at all," Rosy cheeks glowed. I searched for a long time, rummaging through file cabinets in my brain for something to say…

I don't know what made Glory come over to me that day; I never make the first move with anyone. Perhaps it is just difficult to find people that read. But she came back the next day and the day after that. She came and sat on my table with me. Very rarely would we say anything in that time, we would just read in comfortable silence. Like tortoises hiding in our shells. There really is nothing like finding someone that you can sit in silence with. There were conversations, lots of them but I keep them for myself. I haven't seen Glory since she left for university. Like a leaf swaying in the breeze, she eventually fell off of her small apple tree and was blown into the wind. The scraping wind. Covetous thirst- inevitable…

By the time we reached college, we were inseparable. I remember opening our acceptance letters together and screaming like the little girls we were, with excitement. Holding our letters in hand, we mus have looked exactly the same, except of course that she is a foot taller than me.

"I am being poisoned by bread and water," Glory would say. It is difficult to put into words because it didn't happen all at once, it happened gradually: the narcissism that began to fuel her. I couldn't tell if her air of infallibility was her greatest strength or greatest weakness. She was more effervescent than ever; brilliant, intelligent, she burnt so bright that her peers had to cover their eyes when she was around. She studied meticulously hard for Maths, Literature, Biology, Dance, she even played and excelled at the cello in her own time. What was better is that she did it all in the guise of a dandy. She would tell people that she never worked at all, would tell people that she spends most of time watching television or reading satire, that things 'came naturally', she was envied. I suppose, the more that she excelled, the more of a gap she put between herself and other people. She became colder as her peers snarled and whispered derision behind her. I think that the colder hearted beasts in Glory's life thought that the change in her was for the better, that it was important for her distinguish herself from the rest of us. It is true: she became more productive, more directed, stronger, confident. However, she started to become scornful of books that we both used to whimsically enjoy. Lewis Carol became a joke before long. The light that good hearted and innocent thoughts would elicit was extinguished.

"The empty words of a juvenile drug addict is as much a waste of my time as waiting at the bus stop!"

Glory never used to worry about the time. Life would unfold and she would be a part of it, like she was some unique building block of the universe and space time couldn't exist without her presence. As she got older, she started to try and bend it to her will and control the passing of time. No longer a leaf in the breeze but trying to control the wind itself.

I started seeing Glory more as she tried to do something different form the crowd, as she tried to 'breakout'. I guess we were teenagers looking for an experience; I just wanted to be with my friend. She started to invite me to parties, we called them parties. However, looking back, it was a venue for barely legal (and often underage) drinking to take place. Predators lurking. Older guys with cars. Half-witted fools trying to convince half inebriated girls that they had some semblance of intelligence. It was a farce. I could see that the first time that I was there.

Smoke poured languidly through the door like the smoke rising from a crack head's pipe. Some bottom dweller grows what pathetic chin hair they can in some half-baked stab at masculinity. The little cockroach wears his cap at an unconventional angle, gets behind a record and presses 'play'. Without this small stab at individuality and power, with no discernible skills or talents, this insect would no doubt lounge with the other insects. No path, no discernible path, just the vague notion that bravado can be a substitute for identity. Not that this parasite is capable of articulating these thoughts, like a baby that sucks on a teat, the thought pattern is little more than testosterone fuelled impulse that if verbalised would sound: 'Be DJ= Get laid'… The smell of sweat and alcohol is ubiquitous and makes me wonder if there is a smoke machine at all or if the cloud is just a mass of adolescent by-product. Only in the foyer and this is already unbearable.

"I can't possibly go in there," my little horror-struck face said more than my words could have. Drunk people staggering past us- almost knocking us over.

"Katrina, just remember what I told you. You are 17, nearly 18! Experience is knocking at your door! To take anything less than everything would be a travesty to your life and character!" Her voice gets louder as the beat of the overbearing song gets louder.

"Glory, this is hard," my voice is breaking like the scratchy sound of the subwoofer and I feel my eyes welling up as I stood on the verge of I-know-not-what.

"Look at me Kat!- No, stop- look at me. I need you to be brave for me Kat. I know you don't want to, but remember what I said: 'No one knows you are not brave unless you say it! You are not going to admit it to them, you are not going to admit it to me, and you sure as hell are not going to admit it to yourself! -So, Kat, how are you feeling?"

Consumed.

"...I feel fine."

"Then follow me."

Into the darkness I followed. I sank my fears into the night and sailed on through stormy skies. I found that most of the terror and fright was fabricated by a thrill of the unknowing. Most of the evening was spent standing around and not saying a lot. People kept approaching us and offering us alcohol, we obliged once but didn't want to lose sense and personally, I never enjoyed the taste of it. The conversations that could be conjured, the half-hearted and half-witted conversations that could be struck were often hard to hear and with socially awkward teenagers, like ourselves, that didn't really have a lot to say. One man had rather too much to say, but I think that was the effects of the alcohol. I could see Gloria's fine veneer peeling off with every frustrating conversation. With every new suitor she became more reserved, less sharing and more defending herself.

"I am starting to think that this is a waste of time," She looks down her nose at her hands as one does when confronted with the less-than-satisfying nature of one's own work, "This is not the kind of night that I had envisioned. I thought I could find company that resembles Gatsby but all I have found is Mice and… Rats… it should be at great detriment to my future endeavours to call the company 'men'. It should be at great detriment to my own femininity to call any of these people 'ladies'. It was at this moment that Gloria lifted her head, which must have weighed considerably at this point, and caught the eye of a young man from across the room. Quite alone, he looked comfortable in being so and quite about his sense. His eyes, flitting around the room in no particular hurry, caught Gloria's gaze and in that brief moment his eyes widened ever so slightly and he grinning momentarily. There was wild curiosity being bounced from one side of the room to the other, only to be returned in equal measure, if ever so slightly less from Gloria. Maintaining his wistful gaze, he picks up his drink and approaches.

"Hey, my name is Michael, what is yours?""

"Michael?" I stare at Katrina with disbelief and the shrillness in my voice no doubt gives me away.

"Yes, Michael," Katrina repeats, "It is why I hesitated to tell you this story to begin with." Katrina's voice sounds sodden and bare, where it had so much reserve about it before. I have become quiet and submissive and it is she who holds all the power.

"It is okay… it just came as quite a shock..." A sudden pang of disbelief washes over me and the world around me disappears into darkness as I sink into thought.

Michael and Lizzie

"You know I don't care for flowers lizzie," Michael broods briefly before tossing the freshly picked flowers down by his side like a rag doll in the arms of a child that has picked it up one more time than he found it charming and now it will never be loved again. My heart sinks and smiles sag a little, but the sheer magnitude of Atlas stands fast and keeps it up. I feel like I am frowning but I know from experience, from practise that I am still smiling, and the illusion is not broken. The thin ice that is our equilibrium is not broken so long as I smile and pretend that everything is alright. Every slight; dejected petty act of juvenile insolence, rains down on my countenance and I sag and sift through this mud that has built around my ankles. Please don't go, please don't go away, you get further from me with every day and I struggle to keep up, I don't think I have seen you face in so long, I just want one more look at a man that I thought I once saw in a half shattered visage, reflected with the narcissus flowers in a lake that we only visited once.

"Where did you even get them from?" Michael fires again. He never checks to see if his weapons are loaded or if the safety is on.

"What do you mean?" I retort. Why does he want to know where the flowers are from? Can he not just be happy that flowers exist, and that someone loves him enough to pick him out five or six beautiful examples with personal resonance? Just be happy that that someone saw a dark blue flower and thought 'that one flower really reminds me of Michael. The way the fragile stem contrasts the vibrant and violent vehemence of the depressed blue captures Michael rapture perfectly, I think that when he sees it, he will see just how well I know him. How well I have been paying attention to our relationship and he will see that I am the centre object that he oscillates around and instead of looking all around for me, he shall look into the centre of what it is he revolves and be satisfied with what stares back.' But he won't look at me. He hasn't looked at me since the first time we met; I don't feel like we have seen much of each other since then.

"You know what I mean. There is no tag, and it is held together with flimsy paper"

Flimsy paper…

"I picked them. They were wild." My voice, I am trying to project a stern confidence, but hysteria is seeping through the cracks. I remember the thin ice of equilibrium and jerk my neck back up and smile such a forced smile that my bared teeth shine as bright as hospital walls.

"Wild flowers? I have never seen wild flowers growing in this town, where did you go to find wild flowers?"

"Well, some of them are picked from outside people's gardens- "

"There it is! Gardens. You stole flowers from outside people's gardens."

"I didn't steal anything!"

"Then what word would you use lizzie?"

"I don't know, stealing is for personal benefit and I did it for your benefit, so… I don't know. Whatever people call stealing for someone else," My words trickle away from me. I wave goodbye like children skipping to school.

"Stealing, I reckon."

I wish that he could just be happy that flowers exist and that he can enjoy the miracle of them.

My state of clear glass shatters into angel dust.

Outside, the air is crisp. Wrapped with fur feeling at my face, my down turned nose is exposed and the stiff breeze carries small knives. It is a busy street; lights flash into my eyes. The smell of roasting chestnuts is in the air. I have never eaten a chestnut but I know exactly how they smell when they are roasting. I suppose that embodies the entire holiday season. Pining over things that we have no desire to use. I know nothing of Jesus Christ and I don't believe that God has any plan for me. I think my picture of God is nothing more than a child, holding a world full of broken things. I may be a child, especially in the eyes of the universe but… When I look at Michael, I can't help but think that I am holding on to something broken. Which would make the distinction between myself and God is that God is capable of holding a great deal of broken things at once. Chestnuts. Even my one broken thing, I can feel slipping through my grasp, one moment at a time. Like tears, falling through my fingertips.

Michael hails down a taxi. We spend most of the journey in silence. We hold hands and every time we look at each other, we smile. It makes me feel a little warmer for a moment as he squeezes my hand a little tighter. The feel of his hand, delicately caressing mine… Skin like velvet, every movement is responded to and Plato could not guide conversation with such meticulous passion. If I caress his index finger with my thumb, then he will delicately stroke the underside of my thumb and so with the smallest of movements, we dance. We are enamoured. Every small movement is making love and I am lost in the eternity of the moment. His eyes, always looking and scolding me, now look that that of a little boy. Brittle. Without prejudice. My eyes and his, locked in an undying and perpetual act of perfect unison. Our hands, our eyes, our souls... All joined. And we dance, the only thing moving is our hands, in the smallest and subtlest and most precise of movements. Our eyes dance without moving. As each moment stretches and etches its self across the stars, I fall deeper into the rabbit hole. Become consumed in a moment that takes hold of my mortality and elevates it. My soul dances in a great hall and the only two guests are me and Michael.

I don't understand how a love so tender could be so harsh. I am sitting in a very large and eloquent restaurant in the heart of town. It is expensive to eat here. Perhaps my thoughts and feelings are inconsequential to him, perhaps he wishes that I was someone else. Because it does not seem to make the slightest difference how many times I tell him... I feel uncomfortable around people that only value money and their position within society. Michael tells me, "That is what I love about you," as if my thoughts and feelings are that of a petulant child, like I am an accessory. Michael wanted to eat somewhere he felt comfortable and decided that he would like to be entertained while eating, so he brought me out of his bag, wound me up and sat me in a chair opposite him so that he could see 'what he loves about me'. I cannot stand to spend time in the company of this capitalist and egotistical trash. And Michael continues to insist.

"You don't look like you are having a good time," Michael's tone is overbearing, like that of a disapproving father. I feel like I am a child, fighting against destitution.

I try to smile and though my lips move my eyes find it hard to continue the lie. His countenance isn't moved by my inept deception, "I am having a good time, I just feel a little ill."

The ching of champagne glasses is in the air, unbottling of fizz and every now and again. Above the roar of the self-congratulatory breeze, can be heard the haughty laughter of a woman who is considerably more pleased than the last. I duck to avoid a cork that seemed to explode just above my head and look side long at three or four different pictures unfolding…

An elderly gentleman from three tables over looked me directly in the eye and I distinctly saw him grimace. Is there something wrong with the way I look? Perhaps he knows that I do not belong here… I don't belong here with these people. They can smell me. Like one crippled and rotting nectarine slowly blighting the rest of them. Dogs tracking a foreign entity in their field. I can't afford to be here. I can see the crocodiles and the dull toothed alphas: primitive, dull-thinking machines.

"Would you like a drink my dear? You look a little on edge," Michael's voice rings true in a perfect guess and I pull myself a little straighter. I don't trust Michael. I don't think he has a negative agenda; I just think that his perspective is so intrinsically concerned that he might be incapable of loving another human being. His generosity, demeanour, lavish nature stems from looking at life in a cold and calculated manor and concluding that life is easier when people like you. Doors open when you smile at people. Catch more flies with honey than vinegar. Well, you catch more sex, more 'milk of human kindness' with smiles than… vinegar. It all seems so false, so mechanical. I ponder if I am any different. I like to remind myself that I am not such a machine because I cling to the idealistic nature of love. The idea that I can move and act and make decisions based on nothing but a feeling, but a notion that relies on no conscious reason- just an impulse and a provincial, authentic craving to follow it. I like living by uncertainties; chasing ideals that I have yet the impulse to chase. I don't want to stick to the walls of experience but dance in the centre of the ball room. I want to experience love and feel at peace. I set thoughts in motions that collide with action, the thoughts seem impossible in the beginning and they would never keep my soul clean. I met a man and I hoped that we might fall in love. We could create love, together, and live in its impossible nature- that swirling, perpetual kaleidoscope of colour. Greens, humming purple, lava red, gold and silver. Anyone who set eyes on it would be in awe and we could show it to people! People would be inspired and know that love is real and can be created from out of the shadows. Light can come from the darkness… no one would ever have to be alone again. But. This man Michael, he doesn't seek to create anything outside of his compass. He knows only of money and friends and he knows of the darkness. He knows of the charcoal days and the hazy grey, sleepless nights. But he has never seen the light from the dark. He sees the darkness as a one-way, two-dimensional path. He is good enough to people to ward them away from the path. Michael has never seen love in the darkness, he wouldn't believe in it even if he had seen it. His mind, his love is elsewhere. He has corrupted himself. Become darkness and stagnated in it. I see that Michael shall not love.

Not now; not me.

I guess I don't know if I want a drink or not. Michael wants me to have a drink; I don't want a drink. I would have a drink, to help create a beautiful memory with him, start to mix the colours of memory that could create the colours and shades that could be our love. But Michael doesn't believe in those shades, it is all one colour to him.

"I don't want a drink," The thought that created the voice quivered but the voice was regal, confident, stately. "Just a diet lemonade or diet coke please, you know what I like," and I smile my best flattered smile, Audrey Hepburn smiling at a puppy.

"I know…" he doesn't seem to understand. But I don't try to help him and offer no explanation. He doesn't deserve his character slighted and I don't want the backlash of telling a person that he is unsalvageable.

The night continues to rumble on. Dull echoes of distant laughter can be heard from some far end of the restaurant. All but finished now, I sit in front of my second vodka and diet lemonade. Once the room got a little quieter and the music became a little more amiable, the pace slowed and my thoughts began to pool. Michael is currently sipping on his sixth beer with the steady pace of a marathon runner that is in no particular rush to finish but is happy to carry on his escapade until it finishes. He tends to say wat he really means when he is fatigued from his efforts in inebriation. At least, I get different answers.

"Do you love me, Michael?" A small question. He often tells me so but often I think they might just be words.

His answer stumbles in his stupor, "In all honesty, I don't really know what that means, the question is without meaning." 'Without meaning'; without forethought. My I try and estimate the nature of love through the spread of bed sheets.

"How can the question be without meaning? Surely, you know if you love me or not? It is a feeling…" I have trodden this same path before, I recognise the footprints as mine own but they drag slightly on the way out.

"It means I like you. I enjoy your company. You are fire and I enjoy basking in the warmth you radiate. You are lightning and as you flow through my veins, I feel alive. I feel ecstasy, for you. If that is what you mean by love, then yes, I feel love.

"No, love is different. It is a tenderness; it is caring more someone else than yourself. Extreme affinity; a longing, a merging of souls."

"I am not sure that believe in the nature of the soul," Michael says in staggered recumbence, "I think it is something that religious people tell cattle in order to get them to hand over money.

"Do you believe in anything that you can't see? Or is the whole world bleak and materialistic? How can you believe in love? How can you love me if you don't think that love is real? What is love to you?"

"Wow, that is quite the barrage of questions, my love. Can't you just be happy in passion? Are you not happy? Am I not a good partner?"

"I want to build a relationship of mutual love, so, no. I guess I am not happy if my relationship is a lie."

Michael thought hard upon this and after a while, he said, "I love you Elizabeth".

What hurts the most, perhaps more than Michael's preposterous idea that I would be stupid enough fall upon the words: 'I love you' after he tells me there is no such thing as love. More than the disrespect; that he would lie to me… The moment I heard him say the words, I was encompassed by the moment; what should have been a beautiful indefinite-indice, viewed through a purple window; trapped in a love that I cannot trust.

Then I blink and the moment is over.

If love is a union, and I am loving by myself, then this cannot be love. This must be infatuation. How could I be infatuated by such a base man…

Sitting in the Evening Sun

Such a vein and officious fool I have been. Searching for the ideals, of which, the parameters are so badly tempered that I could not look within their margins. I have strayed far from light and into shadow, not to be judged by the fine and shiny misplaced ideals of foolish martyrs whom delude themselves into thinking that the God of parameters would favour what can be found in the light over what more is hiding in the dark. Hollow pursuit. Morality is subjective to individual, culture. Intelligence- the word means nothing. If you judge a fish by is ability to climb a tree, then it shall always be considered a failure. I am sure that Einstein or a Bronte sister, if asked to build a house or to stack the shelves, would have been labelled immense failures. In fact, it should be a disappointment if, these idols of industry (an ill-defined term) should not go mad, have a full psychotic breakdown or an existential crisis at the reality of the monotony- frustrated and quelled by the sun beating on where they should not be able to see it. Should flowers also be denied the light? Worms denied the earth. Would you deny birds the expanse of the sky? Then why should I be denied free thought? Birds do not fully comprehend the majesty of the sky, yet they live in it, revel in it- be love. Some flowers are more fortunate in their idealism than others, 'light or death!' No compromise. To live in the light or die in the dark. I would sooner die on my feet than live on my hands and knees.

Obsession is a young person's game. So, what is obsessed, cannot be said to be old. Michael, you are old before your time…

This single leaf, fluttering down from the great canopy of branches that hover over head moves back and forth, caught in a breeze. It's edges catch the air and it moves in patterns like a ballerina. Like an artist. It has been contemplating it's leap, it's performance, and like all great artists, that is all it wants- One Grande Performance… Led by and leading the wind. Battling to take away what the leaf has revelled in, to show the wind that the leaf is made of wind too. They accept each other and dance like fading moonlight signalling the end of all things worth having. But the leaf cannot be without the wind and falls to the ground without a sound. It lies motionless but does not complain of the wind. Happy now, to be alone in the knowledge it was once the wind and never to be among the canopy again.

The waning summer sun sifts through the branches and conjures tall, overbearing shadows that race along the emerald carpet. The long black trenches cut through the lighter green and autumn oranges. Small pockets of light- hopeful, self-indulgent and self-insistent, they simmer in their hovels. I spend a lot of time sitting here, talking into this empty, open space. No one ever replies but when I communicate with the water that sits beneath my feet, I can see the ripples of my actions. They look large in the immediate, though the further away they trickle, the smaller they get until I can't see them at all. I can hear the echo, the message of a distant past fading out into nothing. The once bouncy and buoyant memory ceases to frolic and sinks to the bottom of the lake, lost to the reeds and the weeds, smothered and decaying with so many words. So many worthwhile words. Good words. Like screaming in the dark and running in pain, we exert ourselves to our heart's darkest paramours for the benefit of no one. For practise. For Art.

A slight breeze walks aimlessly and alone through the open field, light is spread sparse as time. The breeze meanders so that it would seem to be searching for something. Only God knows what. It's shackles blow violently in the wake of it's own wrath. At once, it hits me. I feel it first on my wrists... my wrists... The thought of my wrists wraps me in a blanket of discomfort. Cold, insipid, languid, it's soft touch gently wraps and raps my skin. I shudder as if I have walked over my own grave. My once peaceful and joyful equilibrium with nature has begun to unravel. Each prickly goosebump is a monument to the internal twisting of terror that grips me. Each tiny interruption to nirvana is a ravaged and grievous wound.

Or is it embellishment? The twisting of my heart is like the comfort of a dear friend standing next to me and with every internal scream, she winces. We were standing silently, looking at each other and there was balance. Now, presently, the screams come more frequently. Each tiny interruption to peace produces a reaction like she has been struck, as she has been struck so often before. No longer seeing eye to eye. My present consciousness serves as nothing but a processor and counsellor to the screaming agony of the little girl inside. Unproductive and insidious, this child has taken over my waking thoughts, though it is so precious. Special, devastating, tragic, harrowing, exquisite and unique- I do not deserve the honour. There doesn't seem to be any design, no rhyme or reason, not that I can see. I just wish that I could take that pain away. I am glad that I could be here to share this pain with her.

It is wonderful to feel alive.

Shadows grow longer. The icy fingers of death elongate and touch everything, causing a shadow to fall over my world where there were no shadows at noon. One such dark finger reaches out and I contemplate putting my hand in it's. But I don't. I touch the soft green grass that resides still beside it. The shimmering golden scene that I was surveying not long ago has turned to a contrast of light and dark and though it is less appealing I do relate to it as much the previous. A gust, intuitively whispers in my ear and what it says disturbs me enough to turn my head. Death is not reaching out to me but rather shunning me. I am the last watcher. The last conscious life overlooking my field. The hooded figure is calling a close to the day. Soon, a cull of creatures that revel in the icy palm of darkness shall take the stage. However, I choose not to watch that performance.

I am going home.

The Train Dream

I am constantly reliving my dreams…

We walk side by side in shadows. Intermittent strips of light reflect on the river, shimmer and dance to their own tune. The moon has been swallowed by the water. It is buried side by side with the artificial light. Drowning.

It is not enough. The night is dark and time pressing. Spirited footsteps through hungry streets moves us further away from some pressing terror; two dimensional doorways tantalise our memory of the salient. We must escape this town; Caste aside our ties. The rising sun shall not herald a new day but like the hoisting of a skull on a murky background, shall deliver us.

We arrive… as you do in dreams.

There is a crowd of hundreds, perhaps thousands of people. The mumbled chirping of thousands of drones rises but falls short of understanding and my attention is focusing on the two enormous trains. Old steam engines; fuelled by coal. Each one faces a different direction. The people are all but finished piling onto one train. They reside in carriages or are packed, standing on large pallets to be pulled. The other is barren, desolate. He does not say anything, just holds my hand with his and smiles.

"It's going to be okay"

Packed like sardines in a tin can, the train splutters into life. We face the second train. Watching the smoke rise, apprehending that the train will take us away, but we do not know where. The panic-stricken lightning follows the tracks of my nerves and ignites fear. I do not know where either train is heading, only that I got onto this train because I was told to. I just did what everyone else did.

The panic is too, much it is like a small buzzing to begin with but as the climax approaches, I feel as if I am being stung incessantly. Malicious thoughts cannot be silenced and the fragility of their life and mine is too much. Like a spector, I am lost. One ant scuttling a different direction to the rest. I jump and with speed, unknown to me I glide across the gulf and attach myself to the back of the other train, hoisting myself onto the empty platform.

I turn around to see that my father did not follow me. I have ostracised myself.

The platform is barren. No carriages, no people, just a flat and empty carriage floating on through the night. It is difficult to see as mist engulfs me. This cold and dense fog clouds my vision and mind.

My left foot moves in front of my right and I stagger steadily. Steering without certainty of my next step I walk for longer than the length of the carriage but still there is ground underneath.

Sturdily, I continue to walk, until I come across a young woman. She appears fixated and the first thing I notice is that she is taller than me. She does not see me. I approach the woman, with caution, but though she is faced half away and half toward me, she does not appear to comprehend my coming. It is only as get nearer that I see that the woman is grey. Made of flesh and looking like stone. The young woman, unblinking, with wild bright black eyes is staring out into the mist. She is almost facing me but does not see me.

"Everything needs a reason to live," whispers a voice from the encompassing shroud.

She carries on looking out into the darkness. An expression of longing clinging to her face and to her eyes. It is as if she is waiting for someone or something to come back to her and though even the empty darkness has told her that it is not coming back, she will not budge. Clinging on to an expectant half-smile, wide eyes beaming with expectation.

I move past her, leaving her forever in suspended animation, wondering eternally, who or what she is waiting for.

I walk for what seems like a long time, until I reach a carriage. It looks rustic, even for a steam train. It has no earthly business being here. A cardinal-lava shade with a burgundy door. This carriage looks like it died a long time ago, it has been raised form a museum, an exhibit- I think it likes attention. Without longing or reason, I open the door, step inside and-

Brightly lit, its guts are that of an underground train. Plastic light. Deserted and dirty. Darkness beckons at the window. I move past the poles and past the door to the next carriage. This next carriage is also empty but there is a clear plastic divider between one half and the next. No way of proceeding but through a small hole in the plastic, just large enough for me to fit through. Just me. I squeeze through the hole and open the door on the other side.

Stabbing wildly- Furiously! The man's eyes are fire. He lunges and I retreat to the back of the train. Shaking. Agitated. Fear knows no bounds and soul wrenching fury creates the only sounds. The wells of passion alive in the man's eyes, peeking out from beneath locks of dirty untamed hair, jux'd only by the poor his raggedy clothes. I doubt that he knows that he holds a spoon. Wielding it like a man that is protecting all that he knows dear, the pity and fear only seem to disappear as I walk past him and his fragile defence.

Into the next carriage, where I find yet another clear barrier, separating one from the other. There is no hole in this carriage, nor would I want one. In the floor is etched splatters of crimson rage. A mosaic of scarlet snow, still wet. Carefully caricatured creations of death marred delicacy, lying beside the horror that sits inside. One bare foot, dry blood lies patiently on top but not beneath. Patterned spots of delicately sputtered rouge scattered up a bandaged leg without wound. The man sits motionless in his wooden chair; a dirty cloth wrapped around him so that he is not bare. His chest is, hairless, A perfect canvas for a puzzle that is a mystery. The man's marred fingers are the dripping tools to which remnants of the artist's work reside. Learning forward, his hands are placed purposefully on his knees. He looks directly into my eyes. Intently staring at me as the stars stare at God. In hate for the eternal burden of their unnaturally long life. Unblinking, unmoving, with such intense heat that those same stars would be reborn with new life, screaming silently for the relief of death. The bandages that cover his eyes bleed profusely. Claret. Stinging, flowing, intense fire that capes and burns, trickling down his form. The man is nothing but blood and bandage and he holds my gaze.

Eternally.

The Black and White House

"Diluted time moves in waves to and from the shore. The tide takes souls at the same rate that it gives them. Lingering on the periphery of what is real and what is not, the sea is as eternal as the God that made it. Fading through the ethereal veil, cloudy water settles and maybe a soul can find peace resting at the bottom of a glass half full.

Wake up Elizabeth."

I feel like I heard a voice calling my name. Distinctive and bizarre tone. I thought I recognised it; it sounded like my Fathers... and my Mothers.

Flutter my eyes open, tentatively as the beating of a butterfly's wings: fire sparks and ignites the air around my path- burns the air that preceded. Disfigured shapes pull themselves together in a blurry apparition of faded countenance and then take solid shapes. My eyes dart around the room. White, opaque curtains let nothing in from the outside. Darkness shrouds the room and seeps in through cracks in the walls, as in a dream or a faraway memory. Filling the room. Filling the empty treasure boxes. Filling the bare closet, its arms stretched out wide, like it was expecting me, or perhaps the doors are so open because they couldn't hold back what was inside. The bedroom door is ajar and a thin strip of light emanates from the hall outside. Tantalising- inviting. Tracing the thin strip of light, I sit up- stand. Though it seems I have slept for an eternity, I glide effortlessly across the room without the slightest hint of fatigue.

Open the door and I am struck by the ferocity of the light that I encounter when stepping into the hall. Hospital lights. See right through me. A thin corridor; an old house. Pictures hang on the wall, though I do not recognise them at all. The wall paper clings to the wall in quiet desperation, in perpetual fear that time is lost. Fearful and shy, cowering and covering it's face from the light that attacks in garrisons of languid regiment. Withered.

My foot falls and makes no sound on the ground as I canvass the perilous doors. All alike. Dark, worn wood. Overbearing and as contemptuous as a snarl. The door handle stretches out to shake my hand with all the eagerness of a hungry business man, to touch, just as cold. I turn, to find the door smiling its contemptuous smile, only with a little more self-gratification this time. It is not the only door in this scene to make a fool of me. Up and down the stairs, through the corridors, front and back- all doors are locked. There is no sign of light from the outside world. Defeated, I slump outside my waking-place door. The door opposite towers tyrannically over me. Ruthless depot; corrupted authority. On that tepid; unfamiliar, lonely ground, I begin to cry. My heavy head falls forward into the accepting embrace of my clumsy hands and the lonely frustration seeps from my eyes and collides with a strange and unfamiliar world.

But not for long. As I sat, desperate and helpless in that half black- half white frame of time, the soundless yet unignorable, overbearing body of the door moved out of the way and I could see what lie on the other side.

A little boy. He is playing with another little boy. They have music turned up real loud; they are playing with trains. They put the trains on the track and watch them follow the path. I feel an affiliation to one of the boys.

Another closed door lies beyond this one, much more compliant than the previous family of doors.

In the next room I find myself. I am seating comfortably, with my legs crossed, talking civilly to a man. Savage. The man's name is Savage.

I remember... I sit there with my legs neatly crossed, talking like grown-ups. But then things change.

Savage becomes oppressive, aggressive and he produces a serrated blade the size of my collar bone. Presently, he is tearing at my clothes,

"Nobody is going to save you and nobody is going to believe you."

I am being forced to my knees. This poor girl is trembling.

Then-Gael. That is the small boy's name- Gael, he is my brother.

I stand mortified, watching the incident unfold in front of me. Frozen in time, like a statue of bronze rusting in the entropy of this moment. Watching this scared little girl lose her innocence. Watching this silly little boy try to save it.

- A rush. A blur! The flak of the carpet almost leaps into the air as Gael's hooves strike the ground in his mad sprint to apprehend the assailant. At the final hurdle, he leaps onto the man's back!

There is a brief struggle. The man with the sharp knife flairs his arms frantically.

Then Gael is on the floor. Bleeding. Wide-eyed. Shaking. His eyes are buoyant sapphires floating in a shallow pool.

"Lizzie," he cries, "Mummy."

And I find myself back in the light and dark house, surrounded by locked doors.

A long time seems to pass as I lay on the floor, reliving what has happened. The series of events that must have taken place to lead to that moment.

Inevitably, though at length, another door somewhere down the hall musters the courage to speak to me. I heard it clear it's voice before it called to me with a purposeful 'creek'. Waving to me languidly, I feel nothing but contempt. Stare in stagnant horror for a little while before reluctantly accepting my fate...

"I'm sorry Lizzie, I am so sorry..." The man's voice breaks into a thousand pieces, comes pouring forward like he was trying to hold back the flow of the Thames with a ball and stick. His sweaty, faded blonde hair conceals his face as he shakes, "I thought I could stop them; I didn't think they would..." And the man breaks into more uncontrollable retching, like he is trying to catch up with a reality that has left him behind.

"Dad, what is it? What are you trying to say?"

I take a step back to see myself wearing my book bag over one shoulder. I had just come back from the library, faint memories of reading Poe and trying to write something clever. I move slightly so that I can survey my perplexed, wide-eyed and concerned expression.

"Dad, have you been drinking? What is the matter?" I didn't look at the time but presently, I can see the empty cans of Special Brew and £5.99 Pinot Grigio bottles by his old, worn, beige arm chair- darker and more stained than it ever lived in my memory. Dad's head remains as bowed as the stuffing in his chair.

I lean in a little closer, my voice is gentle, "Dad-"

The curtains are drawn- he grabs me- and his big, blue shimmering eyes are locked in with mine, "They are taking the house Lizzie, I am so sorry, I tried so hard to stop them," he is mumbling now. Horror, panic protrudes from the black of his pupils, it infects everything and the blue looks so tainted. The decaying ruins of my Father.

"Dad," I muster with some composure, "You are scaring me and you are not making any sense-"

"The house Lizzie!" And with that, he lets go again and turns, barely able to keep his footing as he looks away and his violent sobs begin again.

"I... don't understand, Dad..."

He slumps back into his chair and puts a hand over his face but does not close his eyes, just stares fixedly into his hand, like his was staring into the abyss, "It's gone Lizzie," he whispers but does not move his eyes.

I remember that it was at this moment that I wish that I had said something, anything: 'It is not your fault', or 'don't worry, we will think of something' or even just 'I love you'. But I didn't. I just stared at my Father blankly.

It all happened so fast.

They were the last words that I said to my Father. He didn't look at me again. I watched, a frightened and mute ghost, as he got into his car and drove away. The last time that I saw him... or heard of him for that matter...

Time unbinds and the transition is as easy for me as straightening crumpled metal. I find myself back in my black and white house.

"Are you happy yet!" I scream into the empty walls that pass the message along the the empty halls. I stand with my back pressed up against the cold wall, mimicking the eyes that I saw in my Father on our last day. Everyone always said that I had my father's eyes...

I don't know how much time passed before I acknowledged the sadistic wooden antagonist waving at me from down the hall. At first, I was resolved to ignoring it- forever. However, it would appear that the story can't progress unless the twisted lioness is forced to mentally undress and confess her hideous joylessness. So, I oblige...

Grass. Green grass. Bright green grass. My feet are bare, I furrow through memory to try and recall if ever I was wearing shoes. Serious thought, once stern, is turning to serendipity as all I can sense is that sweet, caressing, plump and bashful blades of grass stroking at the side of my feet. The budding group of friends must be celebrating and working together to support me. What quaint and beautiful life to think so selflessly. I wish I should be a thousand times smaller so that I may thank each and every one of them for being selfless bundles of enthusiasm! Or perhaps it isn't me that they are reaching out for but rather they were just stretching out to say, 'Hi' to the sun, which has been brazen and proud enough to stand centre stage in the middle of this exquisite scene. I should hate very much to be a nuisance to the little life that I am coming to think so fondly of, I decide to get a move on, as to not interrupt the conversation of the grass and the sun any longer. The sun seems to understand the embarrassment that I feel at my slight intrusion and smiles straight at me, reassuring. The breeze is the sun's voice and though I can't understand the message, I know it must be a wonderful message because the breeze is soft and warm- I feel it tickling my face and pulling me through the garden. The rose bushes are taller than any I have ever seen. They are in full bloom and I can almost hear them singing,

"Where have you been?"

And I think, "it doesn't matter now, I'm here."

As I come to the end of this secret place of bliss, I smile to the roses that welcome me so invitingly and I am confronted by reams of blue and green and red bunting, streamed around the edges of trees. The decorations are as moss, growing on all that they can rest their feet on. Not just trees and bushes though, the bunting has grown so bold that it has begun to grow on tables and chairs. They are all meticulously decorated with coloured, paper tablecloths - more vibrant intrusion to an otherwise peaceful world. The figurines sitting on each table look so tranquil, so patient, they look proud to be the creation of their maker. The maker can't be far as my ears are greeted with the low and gentle rumblings of laughter echoing from the surrounding trees. Perhaps the trees are saving the laughter for their own parties (and there can be no doubt that this is indeed a party). Searching a little further, I find that I recognise none of the members that I am acquainted with at first. They all seem perfectly happy to be here though. I dart between older gentlemen in tweed suits, I dodge the little girls racing by in their bright yellow summer dresses- they are going to get them muddy! And it will be such a chore for their parents to wash. But to take away the smile from a child? I should volunteer to do the washing for them if it meant the child gets to keep her smile.

A woman brushes past me, long dark hair climbing down her back, and before her, precedes a confident smile of her own- distinguished. She walks tall and makes eye contact with several guests and smiles her confident smile at them without stopping to make small talk. She doesn't make a sound or even seem to break stride as she moves effortlessly between the crowd. An eloquent countenance that embraces a comforting and welcoming pride. Captivated, I follow the strange woman. She finds her table and she has a special smile prepared for the young man who she sits next to on her table. The young man is too young to be her partner, in fact he couldn't be older than 16 or 17. He smiles back with child-like curiosity, wonder- adoration. It is his birthday. He has a badge. The badge says 'HAPPY BIRTHDAY GAEL'.

I absent mindedly stand in front of their table as a crowd begins to assemble. A much older woman appears and greets the woman I have been idolising these past moments, they greet with familiarity before moving on and hugging 'Gael'. A cheer erupts. I turn. The crowd parts and a slight man juggling a birthday cake comes galloping into the scene. White frosted icing and colourful writing. The man takes his eyes off of the icing and looks up, right through his clean but ever fading blonde hair and fixes his jubilant gaze on the birthday boy. What a joyous and bright smile. His eyes are so vibrantly blue, they would shine against the sky. His skin is so clear... He puts down the cake in front of Gael and rushes around the back in one of those comical 'Dad runs' that doesn't move any faster than walking. He wraps his arms around his family, looks up, smiles for the picture. And Gael blows out the candles.